Raoul
More Easily Ignore Evangeline
In The Darkness . . .

. . . But he was wrong. He caught the sweet, delicate scent of honeysuckle. Another faint aroma drifted indistinctly to his nostrils. Her scent. The earthy, delectable scent of *his* woman. It was an elusive essence, but it made him remember long, hot Louisiana nights when the air had smelled of damp earth, crepe myrtle and magnolia trees, of honeysuckle and wisteria. He'd lain with her, and they'd made love in the slanting silver-white moonlight.

He remembered too clearly the way her mouth had been soft and sweetly giving against his, the way her body had fit his perfectly, and the familiar memories stimulated masculine reflexes despite his aching exhaustion. She tempted him as no other woman could. Dear God . . .

She exhaled softly, her breathing gentle. She was as undisturbed by his presence as he was violently disturbed by hers. He lay there, shivering and wretched, his only thoughts for the woman beside him who seemed to breathe more gently, to sleep more easily, now that he was near. . . .

Dear Reader,

June is a terrific month. It's the time of year when the thoughts of women—and men—turn to love...*and* marriage. Not only does June mark the beginning of those hot, lazy days of summer, it's also a month with a fantastic, fiery lineup from Silhouette Desire.

First, don't miss the sizzling, sensational *Man of the Month, The Goodbye Child* by Ann Major, which is the latest in her popular Children of Destiny series. Also in June, look for *The Best Is Yet To Come,* another story of blazing passion and timeless romance from the talented pen of Diana Palmer.

Rounding out June are four other red-hot stories that are sure to kindle your emotions written by favorite authors Carole Buck, Janet Bieber and—making their Silhouette Desire debuts—Andrea Edwards and Amanda Stevens.

So get out those fans and cool down...then heat up with stories of sensuous, emotional love—only from Silhouette Desire!

All the best,

Lucia Macro
Senior Editor

ANN MAJOR

THE GOODBYE CHILD

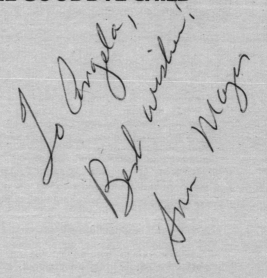

To Angela,
Best wishes!
Ann Major

SILHOUETTE *Desire*®

Published by Silhouette Books New York

America's Publisher of Contemporary Romance

SILHOUETTE BOOKS
300 East 42nd St., New York, N.Y. 10017

THE GOODBYE CHILD

ISBN: 0-373-05648-6

First Silhouette Books printing June 1991

All the characters in this book are fictitious. Any resemblance to actual persons, living or dead, is purely coincidental.

® and ™: Trademarks used with authorization. Trademarks indicated with ® are registered in the United Patent and Trademark Office, the Canada Trade Mark Office and in other countries.

Printed in the U.S.A.

ANN MAJOR

is not only a successful author, she also manages a business and runs a busy household with three children. She lists traveling and playing the piano among her many interests—her favorite composer, quite naturally, is the romantic Chopin.

This book is dedicated to Tara Gavin, my editor.
This story owes its very existence
to her gentle guiding hand.

Prologue

It was raining, and the wind had dropped to nothing. Evangeline Martin looked up impatiently at her lifeless sail and then at the thick fog bank up ahead. White plumes were rolling over the wide Mississippi and silently blanketing everything.

Suddenly she was afraid.

She should never have taken the boat out on a day like this. No matter how awful she'd felt about what *Grand-mère* had done.

"Mon dieu," she sighed, utterly miserable, fighting tears that always came so embarrassingly easily.

She was heartbroken.

She was furious.

Less than an hour ago, her grandmother had offered her irrefutable proof that Eva's fiancé, her adoring Armand, was not twenty-two as he had claimed. Nor was he a medical student at Tulane. No, he was twenty-seven years old, and he had a pregnant girlfriend in Baton Rouge. Another scoundrel of the first order—this one with a prison record—who had been after Eva for her money.

She could sure pick them. Or rather she couldn't. That was the problem.

"You're too softhearted, *chère*. Too sweet and trusting," her grandmother had said, attempting to console her. "You always let men who need you pick you."

But *Grand-mère* was wrong. Eva had chosen him because he'd seemed so proper, and she'd felt so sure her wealthy, conventional family would approve of him. She was the baby of the family, and even though she was in college, they still treated her like one. She wanted to do something right for once, but this was the third time she'd chosen the wrong man. The third time her family had hired a private investigator. Eva was disgusted with herself for always failing them.

She sipped the last of her diet cola and tossed the empty can into the cockpit. She heard a splash and quickly glanced into the cockpit. The can floated beside her life preserver in a pool of water. The plug was gone! The cockpit was rapidly filling. Even as she fought panic and tears, she told herself not to worry. The boat had flotation.

The boom swung lazily across to the other side of the boat and she ducked. Then the sail flapped and was still. The icy rain fell more thickly. The boat was dead in the shallows under the lee of the levee. At this rate she would never get home.

Eva shivered. She'd forgotten the pants to her foulweather gear, and her legs were drenched. She pulled up her yellow, waterproof hood to cover her hair, and considered her dilemma. She felt safer near the shore, but if she didn't steer the boat into deeper water where the current was stronger, where the trees and levee didn't block what little air there was, she'd never get home.

She warily nudged the tiller. She had sailed upwind against the current; she would drift sluggishly toward the bayou and home.

A green-and-white buoy that marked the edge of the shallows slowly slid by. She was in deep water now, the most dangerous part of the river because of the river traffic. She heard the eerie sound of a foghorn somewhere downriver.

Her tiny boat glided by the von Schönburg oil docks and refinery. A huge barge was tied up there. On the other side of the river, hidden behind the levee, was an alley of live oaks leading to Sweet Seclusion, the tumbledown, white-columned plantation house that belonged to Raoul Girouard.

All her life her family had warned her against the Girouards, especially Raoul. They said the Girouards had never been a proper southern family. They had a long history of spawning pirates and river gamblers. But Raoul was the worst of them all. He was such a scoundrel that he was even an outcast among his own family—his father having thrown him out years ago for trying to seduce his young stepmother.

According to rumor, Raoul had only grown wilder after that. He'd become a gambler, a womanizer, a mercenary who would sell his own soul for money. He'd been expelled from every college he'd ever attended. He'd been a merchant marine and a soldier of fortune. He'd lived in Africa like an Arab, taken a trek across the Sahara on a camel and written a book about it. When he'd finally settled down, had he chosen the proper sort of career? No, he'd gone to work for an impoverished prince, Otto von Schönburg, and infuriated all the gossipmongers of the neighborhood, who staunchly believed all scoundrels should suffer, by making both himself and his royal boss filthy rich in the spot-oil business. A gambler's business, *Grand-mère* said. She said as well that no matter how high Raoul lived, his bad character would bring him down in the end. Eva had listened to these stories spellbound, never admitting even secretly to herself how blissfully, sinfully fascinating Raoul Girouard sounded.

Eva's boat drifted into the fog bank, and she couldn't see either shore. She heard another call from a foghorn, closer this time.

Out of nowhere came the violent wash of giant props. The water around her was ominously still. She twisted her neck to see, but the mist was too thick. The roar grew louder and louder.

She screamed and pushed the tiller away, but the little boat did not respond.

Then suddenly she saw a sleek white wall of aluminum and steel slicing directly toward her through the gray water like an airborne torpedo.

She stood up and screamed, but the big yacht bore down on her.

Only in that last desperate second did the captain swerve, missing her smaller hull by mere inches, but his powerboat's wake caught her boat broadside. Waves sloshed over the freeboard and deluged the half-filled cockpit. The boom swung across and slammed into the back of her head so hard she nearly lost consciousness. The hull jostled up and down, the tiller came loose in her hands and she lost her balance and slid helplessly across the slick fiberglass deck into the river.

She hit the cold water face first. She struggled to stay afloat, but her foul-weather jacket and the currents were sucking her under. A second wave from the powerboat swamped her.

She clawed the water like a wildcat, but she was weak and dazed from the blow to her head, and gagged on mouthfuls of water.

Above, the fog layer was thinning, and she could see blue sky. The powerboat was circling and coming back, its big engines cut to a purr. A tall dark man was diving in.

Her last thought was that he was too far away. He would never reach her in time. Still, she swam toward him desperately, struggling to stay afloat and to keep her head above the icy water, but the current was pulling her under. Darkness pulsed around her. She stretched her hand toward him and kicked wildly. Her fingertips touched his briefly and then fluttered helplessly away as the current pulled her deeper and deeper down into an endless liquid darkness.

"You might as well quit trying, Raoul. She's not going to make it," a young voice croaked uncertainly.

Yes, I am! Oh, yes I am—!

Eva's lips trembled with the effort to shout at the two men hovering over her, but she was too weak even to whisper. Her throat and nasal passages burned. Her stomach heaved. Her whole body ached with exhaustion and cold.

She was in too much pain to be dead!

She was suffocating, dying for a breath of air. Air was so close. So painfully close.

Her eyes were shut, and her eyelids were so heavy it seemed that leaden weights lay on top of them. But she was aware of the warmth of the sun on her skin, of the strong comfort of someone's hard arms holding her, of a firm mouth forcing itself against hers, of hot breaths being rhythmically forced down her bruised windpipe again and again.

"Breathe, damn you. Breathe," a man ordered in a rough, imperious growl that made her want to yell at him. He was so unkind, and he was hurting her—never before in her short pampered life had anyone talked to her like that. But such effort was impossible. He wound his long fingers in her thick hair, jerking her head up once more. She felt his lips on hers again. His mouth was open; so was hers. His fingers ground into her upper arms like iron bands, and she felt him push three relentless drafts of warm oxygen down her throat.

Air! At last! She was desperate for it. She gulped it in and then gagged on the vile water coming up from the opposite direction.

She struggled frantically to open her eyes. She was gasping, spitting up water, drowning all over again, and breathing in great gulps of air despite the pain in her throat and her waterlogged chest. Every nasal passage in her head felt enflamed.

His arms still around her, he helped her lean back against plump cushions.

"Pierre, get more blankets. Bring brandy."

This man with the rough hands and voice didn't ask; he commanded. And she'd never put up with that from anyone.

"Where am I?" she whispered, her voice a thin, trailing sound.

Talking was difficult. Her throat still felt paralyzed. Every muscle was cramping from the cold.

Her rescuer didn't bother to answer. "You little idiot, what the hell were you doing in the middle of the river in a sinking boat where you could have been killed? Don't you know that a barge could have crushed you? Barges can't stop on a dime the way I had to."

She was so tired, too tired to fight him. "I'm not as stupid as you seem to think!"

"That's not even debatable."

"You're impossibly rude."

"Because you're impossibly stupid!"

She snapped her eyes open and her mouth, too, intending to issue a passionate rebuke. He was a blur, but what she saw of him took her breath away. He was the most beautiful human being she'd ever seen. A Greek god, with jet-black hair, chiseled features sculpted of bronze, and a body of muscle and sinew as perfect as his face. He had a beautiful mouth. It was wide and sensual, and somehow very kissable.

She had a weakness for beauty. And apparently for kissable mouths.

She rubbed her eyes, and he was still there, her vision of him clearer. He had magnificent black eyes, and they were ablaze with fury.

"The wind died," she managed. "I couldn't sail. If you know anything about sailboats..."

His hard gaze bore into her. "I know a great deal about sailboats, and yours was being sailed by an idiot."

She glanced nervously away. She was on board his yacht, alone with this virile, hostile stranger. "I—I was trying to drift downstream. To get home."

"Where's home? Who are you, anyway?"

"Eva . . . Martin."

He cut her off. "So you're the scatterbrained baby of the, er, illustrious Senator Wade Martin's family."

"Scatterbrained! I'll have you know—"

His derisive gaze began to make a slow, assessing sweep of her, traveling down her throat, over the lush curves of her breasts. She was unaware that her wet white shorts were almost transparent. But his burning eyes made her aware of some new danger.

"I'm not scatterbrained! And I'm not a baby! I'm twenty!" She heard herself, appalled. Just saying her age made her seem so much younger.

"All of twenty?" His knowing smile was cynical. "I'm Raoul Girouard. I'm afraid your family doesn't like me much."

"I'm beginning to see why." She was never, never this rude to anyone.

"Really?"

"My grandmother's told me all about you."

A shadow passed across his handsome face, but he said smoothly, "Then she probably told you I eat little girls like you for breakfast." His voice was soft and low, but it vibrated through every feminine cell in her body.

She regarded him with dark suspicion, her brow so puckered with worry that some of his anger seemed to leave him. The kissable mouth actually smiled.

"Then for midnight snacks?" He laughed softly and, like his voice, his laughter was a dangerously pleasant sound.

Her lips quivered as she tried to suppress a smile of her own. If he was a scoundrel, at least he didn't pretend he wasn't.

"And so I do," he murmured with a sardonic grin. "But you're perfectly safe. I'm not hungry at the moment. I had a late lunch, and it's still the middle of the afternoon.''

His breath stirred the damp hair near her ear as he spoke, and her pulse accelerated in alarm. Some part of her knew that she could never feel perfectly safe around a man like him.

Fortunately Pierre returned with the blankets and brandy. Raoul took the blankets and almost fiercely pressed them around her, molding them to the shapely contours of her body. When he was done, Raoul commanded Pierre to steer the yacht toward Martin House. Pierre vanished again, and Eva was left alone with Raoul.

Raoul held the glass of brandy to her lips. ''Here, this will make you feel better.''

''I never drink brandy.''

''Drink it.''

She scowled at him, but he just scowled back. She took a sip, and the stuff burned all the way down her throat, choking her. Almost immediately she went into a paroxysm of coughing.

He slipped an arm beneath her head and patted her back gently and set the glass down.

''D-did anyone ever tell you that you're incredibly bossy?'' she sputtered.

He merely smiled and kept patting her back until she stopped coughing. ''I'm used to getting my way.''

''So am I.''

She saw her boat drifting upside down toward the shallows, and she began to shiver. It suddenly occurred to her how close she'd come to death. His arms were still around her, and when he would have pulled away, she clung to him, feeling ridiculous for her fears. Just the thought of that dark water sucking her under made her terrified all over again. She didn't know if she could ever go near the water again.

At last he let her go. Embarrassed, she pushed her wet hair from her eyes. "I must look a mess."

Raoul's glinting eyes swept her from head to toe.

"But a pretty mess." His voice was huskily pitched. "I see why they keep you under lock and key."

Just the way he spoke made her feel beautiful.

"You probably say things like that to every woman."

"Maybe I never meant them so much before."

"They say you have a way with women."

"They say...." Again a shadow came across his face, and his eyes grew grave.

He touched her chin, lifted it. Yes, she could see some sadness in his eyes—some secret pain. She met the intensity of his gaze and wondered what he was thinking.

"Was it so awful?" he murmured.

"I don't think I'll ever get over it," she admitted. "The water, the darkness of it . . . I never knew before how much I wanted to live."

"Thank God I stopped the boat in time," he whispered.

Then he did a strange thing. He took Eva's slender hands in his and buried his face in them. She felt the warmth of his bronzed skin, the rough texture of his close-shaven cheek. She grew aware of his heavily muscled body thrillingly close to hers. He was trembling, and she realized that this strong hard man had been just as frightened as she had been.

"I was driving like I've lived—too damned fast." He paused. "Your grandmother's right about me, you know. I'm the kind of man a girl like you should avoid."

"I don't always do what *Grand-mère* says."

He studied the tilted stubborn chin, the flame color of her hair. "So I see."

"She told me to stay out of the river."

"You should have listened."

"If I had, I would never have met you." Eva's breath caught in her throat. She had never been so bold. "I— I shouldn't have said that."

"I'm glad you did."

"I never chase men."

"Chasing the opposite sex can be a delightful pastime."

"You are terrible."

"I believe in enjoying life."

"And conceited."

"Impossibly."

"You have a bad temper."

"Horrendous." He smiled sheepishly.

"And the most scandalous reputation."

"Even worse than my temper."

"At least you're honest about it."

"A man who accepts himself is a free man."

Again she sensed a darkness in him that made her wonder. "Is he?" Eva touched his damp hair, ruffled her fingers through it and then drew her hand back in shock.

"Little girls shouldn't play with fire unless they want to get burned," he said gently, but the shadow was there in his eyes.

"This morning I thought I was in love with someone else. Only now... I—I don't know what I want... anymore."

"But I do."

Suddenly she felt his hands on her shoulders. As his head lowered toward hers, she closed her eyes, her stomach felt topsy-turvy with excitement. She was as fatally attracted as a moth to flame.

"You're sweet," he whispered. "Too sweet for a scoundrel like me." Slowly he drew her into his arms and kissed her softly on the mouth. At the touch of his lips, her own quivered. Delicious little shivers traced over her body. Never had Armand, never had anyone, aroused her emotions with a single kiss as he did.

He released her almost immediately, and she sighed in forlorn disappointment.

"I'm too old and experienced for you," he murmured hoarsely in warning.

"How old?"

"Thirty-five. An antique."

"It's lucky that I come from a long line of antique dealers."

She buried her face in the hollow of his neck and, with a glow of satisfaction, she heard the harsh rasp of his indrawn breath.

"Very lucky," he groaned, pulling away, his dark eyes devouring her.

Something elemental seemed to hover in the air, charging it with tension.

"Your family doesn't like me." His swarthy face was a hard mahogany mask as he issued the warning one final time.

"Maybe if you went into a respectable career—like law or medicine..."

"So law is respectable?" He laughed harshly. "*Chère,* you are very young."

"At least my family already knows all about you and won't have to hire a private investigator."

"What?"

"Nothing."

"Do you always live so dangerously?" he murmured. His lean muscled frame stretched out beside her with graceful ease. The sun broke through the fog. Its flooding brilliance caught the side of his face and made the gray at his temple stand out against his black hair.

"Never—until today."

Carelessly he took her hand in his. Just his nearness and his most casual touch caused an emotional upheaval in her.

He was the forbidden. A known scoundrel.

She should get up and run.

But as his hand slid caressingly along the length of her arm, she stayed right where she was.

He made her feel alive in every cell in her body. She sensed a beauty in him that was more than physical.

If he was a scoundrel, she would simply have to redeem him.

One

He had hung up the phone, but he could not forget the call.

So—Otto had found him out, in the nick of time to stave off the ruin of his vast von Schönburg empire. Otto would stop at nothing now that he had learned his enemy's true identity.

The man at the desk had learned that bitter truth the hard way. Beneath his silk dress shirt, there were tangled coils of flesh that ran the length of his back, scars from his stay in a terrorist prison camp. Because of a bullet wound to his left thigh, he would walk with a limp for the rest of his life. But the worst scars were carved like fissures into his soul. Betrayal, prison, the desert—*Africa*. All these tortures he had endured because of one man, Prince Otto von Schönburg.

Now Otto was playing a new deadly game—with the woman Nicholas had once loved.

Nicholas had always known he would have to deal with her someday.

But not like this.

Evangeline was in dreadful danger.

Because of him. Because of that single governing emotion that had driven him since Africa—his fierce desire for revenge against von Schönburg for almost destroying him, for blackening his name; revenge, too, for those men who'd fought under him and died.

Nicholas didn't want his carefully laid plans to get even with von Schönburg blown away because of Eva. He didn't want to be involved with her at all.

He curled his fist into an iron-tight knot of flesh and bone.

But he was.

Just as he knew all of Otto's weaknesses, Otto knew his.

And Evangeline Martin had been one of them from the first moment he'd pulled her from the Mississippi River and breathed life back into her.

Not that Nicholas loved her. Not anymore. She belonged to another time, another world. He had been another man, and she had been part of his foolish dream. The emotion that now filled his heart ran deep, but it was of a darker strain.

He lighted a cigarette and carefully shook out the match. It was Friday before a beautiful European summer weekend. Everyone else had gone home. Even Zak. The trading room on the fifth floor of Z.A.K. World Oil was ominously quiet. The telephones no longer buzzed constantly; the remote-control video screens were blank. During the day the room was a war zone as his agents scrambled for cargoes and markets. Z.A.K. was a key trader in the international spot-oil market.

The man who had called himself Nicholas Jones for the past eight years was seated alone in the dark staring unseeingly out the windows at the quiet Rotterdam neighborhood of centuries-old brick town houses beneath his glass office building. Every muscle in Nicholas's lean six-foot frame ached with exhaustion. He was forty-five. His once-black hair was winged with silver. Deep worry lines grooved his handsome dark face. His expression was harsh and set. His black eyes that had once flashed with youthful dreams were world-weary and cynical, as though cruel experiences in his life had obliterated all softness in him.

He should have known cornering von Schönburg had been too easy.

"Raoul," Otto had whispered in his guttural German accent into the telephone. That dreadful voice. Nicholas had known it instantly. "So you really are alive."

"No thanks to you."

"You're the owner of Z.A.K., the genius pulling the strings of his puppets from backstage. You've done well, my friend." The German voice lowered to a gravelly purr. "Thanks to me. Or rather at my expense. But no more. And to think—once you worked for me instead of against me."

"No more. I put the noose around your neck. I have only to pull it tight to strangle you."

"You still don't get it. I have Evangeline."

Evangeline. He hadn't seen her for eight years, yet at the mere sound of her name Nicholas had gripped the armrests of his chair with clenched fingers. A silence had filled the office—the still, alert silence of terror.

"The noose is around *your* neck, my friend."

"Otto, you listen to me—"

"No, you listen to me, Girouard. You're good at what you do, but you lack the killer instinct. I don't. Last night I held her in my arms. We made love until dawn. The silly little fool thinks I want to marry her. She wants marriage and children. She still wants her family's approval, and who could not but approve the most eligible bachelor in Europe?" Otto laughed. "I was always so careful about my image when you were not so careful about yours. But imagine, me choosing her, an American and a little nobody—even if her father was a senator—when I could have any of a dozen princesses. But she is a very beautiful woman. A delicate, fragile woman. You and I always did have common tastes."

"We have nothing in common, you bastard" came Nicholas's raw, angry drawl.

"Do as I say, or she dies."

"What do you want?"

As if he couldn't guess. Because of Nicholas, Otto was involved in a complex tangle of disastrous deals in the spot-oil market. Otto wasn't getting his money because Pelican Oil had filed for bankruptcy. Other companies weren't getting their money, either, and they were refusing to pay. The feds had just seized six ships. Otto had been a key buyer in each of the multiple chains of buyer-seller deals having to do with the distressed cargoes. Six distressed cargoes meant demurrage charges of more than three thousand dollars a day. Nearly ninety-three million dollars was at stake to be exact. And Otto owed immense interest payments next week on his vast real estate holdings.

"Get on that telex of yours first thing Monday morning, my friend, and get Velmar Oil to pay on those letters of credit."

"I own only a small interest in Velmar. Pelican was the weak link in all those chains. Why should Velmar pay money Pelican owes?"

"It's because of you that Pelican is in trouble. Pay them what you owe them."

"Pelican sold me East bloc oil and didn't deliver."

"Use your influence. Z.A.K. could issue Velmar a letter of indemnity."

So there it was.

"A letter of indemnity when Z.A.K. wasn't even involved?" Nicholas's low rasp rose to a roar. "Do you think I'm mad? You're asking me to ruin my own company, to jeopardize all my own deals, to betray all my contacts, my suppliers, everyone I do business with—I'd be washed up in Europe for good—all this to save you!"

"To save Evangeline."

"She means nothing to me." Nicholas's voice softened, but even that low tone held a steel edge. "We were always wrong for each other."

"You mean a great deal to her."

"You're a liar."

"Maybe. Maybe not. You knew about Pelican. You stayed out of the deals, hoping to lure me into them by tempting me to recapture markets you took from me. It took me a long time to figure you had to be behind Z.A.K. and Velmar, too. There was only one man who could play this game better than me."

"If you thought I was so good, you shouldn't have sold me out in Africa."

"I was in a tight spot. I made a deal. You were expensive. I had to cut . . . costs."

"Cut the throats of my men, you mean."

"Enough said. I can't wait to settle this through the courts."

"Where can I reach you if I need . . . more time?"

"Portofino. *La Dolce Vita*. While you scramble, I shall be enjoying champagne, and sunsets, and . . . your woman."

Nicholas felt the blood rise up his neck. His face flushed as he thought of the two of them together— Eva, always trusting the wrong man, unsuspecting of any danger, completely at Otto's mercy. Otto would tell her all the bodyguards were for her protection. It would never occur to her they would be her assassins.

La Dolce Vita was Otto's yacht. Two hundred and twenty feet of sleek white aluminum—it had been custom made in an Italian shipyard by one of the world's leading designers. It was a floating palace with multiple layers of afterdecks, a pool, a helipad. Its security was impregnable.

"Either pay yourself or get Velmar to pay. If you don't, then Eva dies. London is a very dangerous city. There are cars, motorcycles, bombs. My friend, she's still in love with you."

"The hell you say."

"But that won't stop me from sleeping with her."

The line went dead.

Nicholas held the phone for a long time. Otto was asking him to commit financial suicide to save a woman he hadn't seen in eight years.

What did one woman matter? One life? Nicholas had learned a long time ago just how cheap a life could be. A hundred men had died because Raoul had trusted Otto. Later Raoul had seen more men die as easily as flies, in prison and in the desert.

He leaned back in his chair and ran both his hands through his thick black hair. His tie was loose and the top button of his shirt was undone.

He was determined not to think of her.

Not yet.

Raoul Girouard. His real name. Odd how alien it sounded. It brought back the past as nothing else could. So many years ago he'd gone by that name...yet it seemed a stranger's now. Just as his own past almost seemed a stranger's life instead of his own.

Had he really ever been von Schönburg's man? He had worked for him, yes. Right after the oil embargo when OPEC ripped up all its old contracts and proved they weren't worth the paper they were written on. Spot-oil traders had begun to provide cargoes of oil to countries that couldn't get them through conventional markets. Otto had been just another impoverished aristocrat who'd gotten into the spot-oil business and done reasonably well. Then he'd hired Raoul, and Raoul's brilliance had made him into a billionaire. Otto had invested in everything—from African oil fields to stocks, bonds and art.

Back in those golden years when crude-oil prices soared from less than four dollars a barrel to nearly forty dollars a barrel, a trader could make a million dollars on one deal alone. Raoul had been incredibly successful.

But the good times hadn't lasted. The North Sea had come on-line; U.S. regulation had been stamped out. Things had happened so fast that the oil industry had never been the same since. Now the expense of stock-piling oil inventories had led refiners to rely on the spot market as much as possible.

But the game was different now. Smaller. Tougher. More dangerous. It took more skill to play than it had before.

At the height of his successful partnership with Otto, Raoul had met Eva and fallen in love.

She had seemed a dream. She and her family had represented the kind of loving, stable world to which Raoul had always secretly wanted to belong. His own mother had died when he'd been an infant, and his father had shown him the door when he was barely seventeen. After that loveless start, Raoul had been an angry young man. The anger and the hardship of starting on his own too young had made him do reckless things he later regretted. He'd been toughened, changed forever. Then he'd met Eva, and her softness had almost made him believe he could erase his whole life and start afresh with her. But she had never trusted in him, in the man he was. Right from the start, she'd wanted to change him, to smooth away all his rough edges, and he'd let her try. Until he discovered that no matter what he did, he would never be good enough for either her or the Martins.

He'd been so desperately in love with her, for her sake, he'd even applied to law school. Without a care how she hurt him, she'd broken off their engagement—to spare her grandmother the pain of having Raoul Girouard for a grandson-in-law.

His male pride obliterated because the woman he loved thought so little of him, Raoul had been only too willing to leap at the first chance to get away from her. And that had been Africa.

Because Raoul knew Africa and Arabic, Otto had asked him to go to Rana, a tiny, war-torn North African nation to assess the danger to the newly acquired von Schönburg oil interests there. A nearby terrorist nation had been fighting to seize control of them. Raoul had jumped at the chance, even though at the last minute Eva had begged him to stay.

Once in Africa, Raoul had analyzed the situation and told Otto he would eventually lose his investment, but Rana could probably put up a fight for a year. Otto had used this information to make a profitable, self-serving deal with the terrorist aggressor nation. Not only had he sold his oil interests, but he'd sold the vital intelligence Raoul had given him as well, information that would shorten the costly war from a year to days. The terrorists had moved in fast, trapping Raoul and his men in Rana. Most of them died defending von Schönburg's interests.

Otto, always so careful about his own image, had spoken to newsmen around the world and twisted the truth, telling them Raoul had sold him and all his men out in Africa. These lies had been printed in all the right papers. Otto had emerged blameless and a much wealthier man.

But Otto had made one mistake. He hadn't made sure of his kill.

Not that he hadn't tried.

A man by the name of Nicholas Jones had been shot on that last brutal day. Badly wounded in the left thigh, Raoul had lain beside Jones's body. When Raoul saw the terrorists checking the papers of all the foreigners' bodies, some instinct had warned him to exchange identification papers with the dead Jones.

When the terrorists had found Raoul Girouard's papers on Jones's body, they'd stopped asking questions. Raoul's own face had been bloodied beyond recognition. The terrorists had hauled him back across their border to prison, but not before he'd witnessed Otto's bodyguard and hit man, Paolo, sinking a bayonet into Jones's body.

Raoul hadn't died from his wounds, nor from the starvation diet of the prison camp. Nor from the labor, the heat or the beatings with rubber hoses. He'd met Zak, a black who was half English, half Egyptian. After thirteen months they'd escaped. They both spoke Arabic and knew camels. They'd groped their way across the Sahara from well to well.

Before he'd gone to Africa, Raoul had authorized a Swiss bank to pay the note on Sweet Seclusion, his home on the bayou. When he didn't return in two years, the bank quit paying. It had hurt to learn that Otto had bought Sweet Seclusion on the auction block. But what had hurt even more was the discovery that Eva had helped Otto restore it.

With his name blackened by a scandal so terrible neither Eva nor her family could ever accept him, Raoul had not returned to Louisiana. He'd withdrawn his money from his Swiss account, kept his assumed name and set himself up in business, with Zak as the front man for Z.A.K. World Oil. In the years that followed, deal by deal, Nicholas had worked behind the scenes of his own company to destroy the von Schönburg fortune that he had helped build. Again and again he'd made better deals in the spot-oil market, always working to steal Otto's markets, to get close to Otto's contacts, to hurt Otto at the only enterprise that really mattered to the man—making money. Recently there had been articles in the London papers that the foundations of the von Schönburg empire were crumbling.

Companies like Z.A.K. didn't produce or refine oil; they were middlemen, buying and selling cargoes of

crude that might not be delivered for months, oil that
hadn't even been pumped out of the ground. The right
call meant big profits; the wrong calls meant equally
huge losses.

Nicholas had guessed right so often that there were
those who believed he was infallible.

Maybe he'd been too damned good.

Maybe von Schönburg was right. Maybe all he'd
done was place the noose around his own neck. If he did
what Otto wanted, Z.A.K., and everybody who worked
for Z.A.K., were finished.

Was one woman worth so much?

Otto had said he lacked the killer instinct.

But the man Otto had sent to Africa and betrayed was
dead.

Nicholas Jones was a different breed entirely.

What was Eva like now? The woman Nicholas read
about in the papers attended the smartest London
charity balls, lunched at Harry's Bar, spent late nights
at Annabel's, and took ski trips to Saint Moritz. She
had an expensive antique shop to finance. Otto was
royalty. Did Evangeline want success and status and respect more than anything? The girl he'd known had
wanted love.

Otto and Evangeline. Thank God it was impossible
for him to picture them together.

The only way Nicholas could ever remember Eva was
as she'd looked that day he'd last seen her, that soft
rainy afternoon when she'd driven to New Orleans and
thrown herself into his arms at the airport and he'd
pushed her away. He'd been too furious and disillusioned to listen to her.

She'd been twenty-two with long red hair, great,
dark, tear-filled eyes and a sleek slim body. When he'd

pushed her away, he'd felt as if he'd torn away a part of his body and cast it off. The pain of it had been so fierce, he'd almost relented. Almost. Instead he turned and walked up the ramp to his waiting plane. She'd called after him, but he'd walked on. Whatever her faults, that girl who'd loved too easily and cried too easily, who had never learned she couldn't please everybody had been nothing like the glitzy, social climber he now read about in the London papers.

One thing about her was unchanged—she still had a penchant for picking the wrong men.

Eva had been in London a long time. Nicholas read the London papers, so he'd kept up with her struggle to rise in the art and antique world. He'd even learned of her financial problems. They didn't surprise him—she was too softhearted and disorganized to run an efficient shop.

Otto was an antique collector. Otto and Eva had a thing for antiques. Now it seemed Otto and Eva had a thing for each other.

Otto was a collector—not only of beautiful objects—but of people who fascinated him or who might prove useful as well. It was all too obvious that Otto had kept Eva on the string all these years just in case he ever needed her.

Nicholas's gaze wandered downward to a tree-lined canal where reddish-gold sunlight sparkled and children played in a park. He took a deep, bitter breath.

Eight years was a long time to remember a woman. To remember her arrogant, prestigious family he'd longed to be a part of. To remember a woman who couldn't accept him for the man he was, who couldn't really trust him, who valued her family more than the man she professed to love.

Still, it was odd that the thought of Eva being in danger—and all because of him—made every nerve ending in his body tense with alarm.

Hours later, after Nicholas got back to his flat, he went upstairs to his bedroom. His thoughts kept returning to his telephone conversation with Otto.

My friend, she's still in love with you.

Then why the hell was she engaged to Otto?

Why the hell was she still single at all?

Nicholas yanked open a drawer and pulled out a ring with a black onyx stone and a broken golden chain that sparkled against his brown palm. He had given it to Eva and, when he went to Africa, she'd given it back to him as a symbol of good luck.

It was time he got rid of the thing. He pulled out a black velvet box, black paper and gold ribbon. Then he picked up the phone and dialed.

A woman answered in German; her voice was light, eager. Too eager. Anya was Otto's beautiful, rebellious daughter. Like Otto, Raoul collected people who might prove useful.

"I can't see you tonight, Anya," he said. "Not for a week or two."

"But..."

"I will see you in Portofino at the party you're giving your father."

"What? What of Papa?"

"Pretend we're meeting for the first time."

She laughed huskily. "The danger will make everything more exciting."

He hung up the phone.

Of one thing Nicholas was sure: Otto wasn't bluffing. Nicholas had till Monday to deliver.

Nicholas had to get Eva before then.

Or Otto would kill her.

Two

As always, Eva's shop on fashionable Pimlico Road was in chaos.

Eva had had another of her sleepless nights. She'd awakened, startled from one of her much-dreaded dreams about Raoul. More than anything she longed to forget him, to hate him, to fall in love and marry someone else. But she who had once fallen in love so easily had never been able to love again.

Not after him.

He had ruined her.

He still haunted her.

Not that she would have admitted it to anyone.

Her family had been full of I-told-you-so's. They couldn't understand why she hadn't married. And she couldn't tell them.

After her dream, she had walked her floors till dawn, and the next morning she was tired and on edge. So tired she would have loved to scream or do something else that was equally unladylike.

At the moment her cat was the center of her shop's crisis.

The afternoon was dark and rainy, the streets jammed with traffic. Eva hated rain.

Inside the shop the phone was ringing. Eva hoped it was Mr. Jeffries calling, the fat little man with the wire spectacles and bald head who owned the magnificent, twelfth-century, illuminated manuscript Eva was trying to buy for Otto. Her shop, Connoisseurs, would be in the black if she could negotiate this sale. She hoped Mr. Jeffries had a better price than his outrageous sum of nine million pounds.

On another line, Prince Otto von Schönburg was on hold. Nigel, the shop's manager, had gone to an auction on Bond Street. There were stacks of unpaid bills on Eva's desk. The constant pressure of keeping Connoisseurs afloat was too much for Eva on any morning, but today it was worse than usual.

Why didn't Zola answer the phone? Lady Vivien Balfoure was waiting in Nigel's velvet-walled, beige office for Eva to return so they could haggle over the price of a certain urn made of the finest Sèvres porcelain, an urn that Vivien had coveted for months but Lord Balfoure refused to buy for her.

The front doorbell tinkled. High heels tripped across marble floors and hesitated before some tempting art object. Doubtless, another customer who needed instant service. And the phone kept ringing.

While all this was going on, Evangeline was trapped in the warehouse behind Connoisseurs. There were so many important things clamoring for attention. But first she had to rescue Victor from the jammed drawer of an eighteenth-century armoire made of glowing mahogany and padauk, before she bundled it off to her restorers. He had scratched her twice when she'd stuck her bandaged hand inside and grabbed the only thing she could reach—his fluffy black tail.

What a morning! It had begun at one a.m. with her nightmare about Raoul. Then on her way to the shop a motorcycle had almost run her down in the rain. As a result she had stumbled over a water hydrant and sprained her wrist. Otto kept bombarding her with telephone calls. He refused to discuss the manuscript. Instead he was carrying on about the motorcyclist, saying that he and his family had received death threats because of an arms conference he was to attend. He was demanding that she drop everything and come to Portofino so he could protect her. Tonight!

And now Victor.

Eva leaned down and peered into the drawer. She pulled at it, but it wouldn't budge.

Yellow cat's eyes stared at her from the dark.

"Victor, please...*chère*. Kitty, kitty. The movers are here," Evangeline pleaded in Cajun French, his native tongue, and most decidedly his favorite language.

Victor yawned and showed a mouthful of needle-sharp teeth. Like all males, he loved being difficult. His yellow eyes became disdainful slits. His ears flattened. His black tail flicked back and forth as if to say he hadn't the slightest intention of coming out unless he heard something really fascinating like the can opener. The phone kept ringing.

"Zola! Haven't you found Victor's sardines yet?"

Two burly men with a dolly and furniture quilts shifted their weight impatiently in the shadowy warehouse. Finally one of them spoke in a surly undertone.

"Look, luv, how wuz I ter know 'e was in there when I shut the drawer? But sardines or no sardines, we ain't got all day. Not to wait for no bloomin' cat."

The bad grammar grated, but the casual endearment was unendurable.

"Love!" Every nerve in Eva's body bristled. Very slowly Eva pushed her tortoiseshell glasses up the bridge of her nose. She arose and studied the gum-chewing, tangle-haired hulk lounging against a crate of Venetian crystal. Red letters blazed Party Animal from his black T-shirt.

"You're new, aren't you?" she demanded briskly.

For the first time he looked at her.

Her severe, double-breasted black jacket with white pinstripes, matching pleated trousers and black spike heels accentuated her pencil-slim figure. Her red hair was pulled back. There were touches of gold at her throat and ears. Every detail of her costume, even her overlarge glasses, was deliberately calculated to make her seem more suave and professional than she secretly doubted she could ever be.

But the big boy bought her look of competence. "Give me a break, lady," he muttered, shuffling uneasily.

"Who interviewed you for this job?"

"A...a...Miss Zola."

"I suppose she told you nothing about what to wear to work?"

"Nothing."

"First, I am not your 'love.' I am Miss Martin, your boss. Second and third, no message T-shirts and no gum in Connoisseurs."

The boy gulped his gum. He hung his head.

One party animal tamed. Eva smiled softly, triumphantly.

The phone rang again. Outside it was pouring. Victor still held command of his drawer. Lady Balfoure was still waiting. The sale of the manuscript and the future solvency of Connoisseurs was still very much up in the air, but Eva felt better because she had won this minor battle.

Suddenly Zola flew into the warehouse and waved a can of sardines that flashed in the dim light like a victory signal. "I found them."

"If you'd just put things where they belong in the first place—" Eva began.

"If you'd just leave Victor at home where he belongs—"

They both stopped, each realizing it was useless to try to reform the other.

Zola was black, beautiful and original. She'd come from Louisiana with Eva. She adored antiques. Tall and thin, Zola had prominent cheekbones, huge eyes and a shower of ebony ringlets. She always wore miniskirts and painted her nails to match. She was the last sort of person one would have expected to find in a shop like Connoisseurs. She kept the accounts in a jumble. She forgot to place orders and relay telephone messages. But she loved the customers, and they adored her.

"Now where's Victor—that rascal?" Zola murmured.

"In there." Eva pointed to the armoire.

"I can handle it from here if you want to get the phone, Eva."

"If..."

Zola pushed a pair of lime-green bracelets that looked like huge frosted doughnuts up her golden arms. She

opened the can and held it against the drawer. The
movers were as entranced by the curve of golden thigh
as was Victor by the delectable vapors of sardines.
"Here, kitty kitty," she whispered in a tone that all
three males found utterly seductive.

Eva saw his black paw poke out of the drawer just as
she raced out of the warehouse for the phone. Otto's
line was blinking. She grabbed it.

"*Liebchen,* for a moment I was afraid—" He
sounded tense.

Eva rubbed her bandaged wrist. "You're not still
carrying on about that idiot on the scooter?"

"I won't be able to rest until you're safe with me—
tonight."

"You're just using that to order me to come. I told
you I never go to birthday parties," Eva insisted firmly.

"Not even mine?"

"I explained months ago. And you know how I hate
boats."

"*La Dolce Vita* isn't a boat. She's a palace."

For fifty-eight years Otto had been used to getting his
way. Eva held the phone away from her ear for a minute and took a deep breath and counted to five.

She put the phone back to her ear. "I've been single
too long to put up with this sort of nonsense from any
man—even a prince."

He laughed. "This prince has asked for your hand in
marriage."

"Things were perfect before you became obsessed
with marriage."

"They will be so again, once you marry me. I want
to announce our engagement at my party."

"I—I'm not sure I should marry anyone." She decided to make a joke of her doubts. "Why should I

subject myself to the whims and tyrannies of a husband—even a royal one?'' She was only half teasing.

"Because you are an idealist when it comes to people and money, and I am not. Because I have money, and you need it. Because I am the only man you've dated that your family has ever approved of. Because you want children. Because you are a woman, the kind of woman who can never be complete without a man. Because you get lonely living alone, *liebchen*. I see it sometimes in your eyes. Because, you see, you need me, and I want you.''

He had struck a nerve—several nerves.

She was tired, so tired of struggling all by herself, so tired of trying to prove herself, and failing. So tired of trying to forget Raoul. All she had ever wanted was to marry and be happy.

"If you come, we can discuss the manuscript," Otto purred.

Nine million pounds. Did he think he was buying a manuscript or her?

Nigel had warned her. "Prince Otto buys his wives just as he buys his masterpieces." And after all, there had been three others.

Otto used her silence to change tactics abruptly.

"*Liebchen*..." There was a new element in Otto's voice. "Something else rather unpleasant has occurred. I've had news of...Raoul."

Otto hated Raoul and almost never mentioned him.

She felt a tingle of unwanted excitement as well as a tingle of some new and very surprising emotion—danger. "What?"

"There's a man who says he was with Raoul in Africa when he died."

"Who?"

"You will have to come to Portofino to meet him. I can tell you nothing but his name, Nicholas Jones."

"The name means nothing."

"He says he has a message to deliver."

"I'm not interested in Raoul," she murmured, struggling to keep her voice flat and emotionless.

But in the antique, gilt-edged mirror across the room she saw that her face was as still as death, as gray as ash. Only the frantic pulse in her throat told her she was very much alive.

"The sun is shining in Portofino," Otto whispered.

Her pulse became quick erratic thuds.

"I am offering you a paradise of sun, sea and cobblestones. A mysterious stranger who knows something of my former, treacherous protégé and your 'friend.' What kind of woman would prefer staying in London and working?

Outside the window there was nothing but gray wet.

"It's supposed to rain in London—all weekend," Otto persisted.

Rain always reminded Eva of Louisiana. Of Raoul. Of the girl she'd been so long ago. Of the months of horror and scandal after his death, when all the vicious stories about him had been printed and the local gossips had linked her name to his. Rain reminded her of everything she had run away from Louisiana to forget.

Her pulse drummed like the rain against the window. The dark day coupled with her sleepless night and her approaching birthday must have made her more susceptible to the slightest mention of Raoul. Mr. Jones could say nothing that she did not already know. Raoul was dead, and both she and Otto wanted to forget him.

Still, she'd been working too hard at Connoisseurs. She needed a break.

Doorbells jingled and Nigel bustled into the shop, his weary arms brimming with auction-house catalogues. If she managed to negotiate the sale of the manuscript, no one at Connoisseurs would have to work as hard as each did now just to meet the overhead. Zola could have more time off for her baby.

Sun, sea and cobblestones. Eva imagined the white afterdecks of *La Dolce Vita,* the sparkling sunlight on the Ligurian sea, the warmth of the sun on her own skin. There would be elegantly served lunches on the afterdeck following a leisurely period for gossip and aperitifs. The weekend would be a blur of delectable foods, matching wines and champagne. She hated water sports, but she could watch the other guests sail, ski or swim.

And she would meet Nicholas Jones. Perhaps he could tell her something that would make her stop her inexplicable dreams of Raoul.

When Eva made up her mind, she made it up quickly. "So, it's really sunny?"

"My jet is standing by at Heathrow to pick you up, *Liebchen.*"

"You were very sure of yourself."

There was a silence, and then Otto spoke, his guttural purr triumphant. "Because—you see—you are not so different from other women."

She felt like screaming at him, but he had already hung up.

She slowly set down the phone.

Sun, sea and cobblestones. And Otto's mysterious stranger, Nicholas Jones.

Everyone thought she should marry Otto. Even Nigel.

And she wanted to.

But it would be so much better if she could put the past and Raoul Girouard behind her before she did.

Hadn't she come to London to prove that she could make a life for herself and forget him?

Life was almost perfect when she managed to.

And now this.

She flipped her calendar, intending to see what was scheduled for the next week.

But the page fell open on her birthday, which was the same as Otto's although no one knew, not even Otto, because birthdays, especially her own, were occasions she no longer celebrated. An eternity ago Raoul had sent her a letter and promised to return on her birthday. He had sounded almost like he was ready to make up their quarrel. Instead, on that day, she had learned of his betrayal and death.

She would be thirty. Had Raoul lived, he would be forty-five. She had never imagined she would really ever be this age without a husband and children of her own. Her sister, Noelle, had twin girls. Otto would marry Eva, give her children. The biological clock was ticking.

Beneath the date for her birthday Eva had scribbled a single word.

"Portofino."

Suddenly it seemed that her entire life was hanging in the balance.

Three

———

Nicholas Jones didn't like the heavy damp wind sweeping across the balcony. Nor did he like the purple clouds towering on the southern horizon. A nasty storm was brewing in the Mediterranean, a freak, unseasonable storm that none of the weather forecasters had predicted.

He wasn't sure how to fit a storm in with his plans for tonight.

He put the thought of the storm out of his mind, and focused on the problem at hand. Nicholas felt like a common thief as he crouched in the shadows of the little balcony outside Otto's stateroom, the luxury cabin Otto had given Evangeline.

Otto had armed men everywhere. If they caught him aboard, they'd kill him.

This was hellish nonsense. It seemed like a scene from one of Nicholas's blackest nightmares.

He was insane.

But from the moment he'd spoken to Zola, he'd known he had no choice.

"A motorcycle nearly ran her down. Prince Otto says she's a target because of her close connection to him. He's involved in some sort of international arms conference. She went to Portofino so he could protect her."

Damn the clever bastard. . . .

So here Nicholas was in Portofino, an unlikely hero in an unlikely melodrama, trying to pick what was surely the most stubborn lock in Europe. He could have been enjoying himself on board his own boat, *Rogue Wave*.

Instead his bad left leg was cramping. It was a struggle not to gag on the acrid smoke that blew up from the afterdeck. Beneath him two of Otto's men were smoking cheap Italian cigarettes and regaling one another with the filthiest jokes Nicholas had ever heard.

Carefully Nicholas placed a black-and-gold box beside the door so that both his hands would be free. Then he inserted the tiny knifelike tool back into the lock and began to jiggle it. He had to work fast before Otto came upstairs.

Nothing happened.

Noxious smoke enveloped him before the wind blew it away. Perspiration beaded his brow. Twin howls of laughter erupted over a particularly lewd item. Nicholas was too old for this game; he didn't know any of the rules or the tricks.

But he had to see Evangeline alone to try to talk her into going into hiding. He couldn't risk a public meeting.

Since she believed Raoul was dead, there was no telling what she would do when she first saw him again.

Nor did he have the slightest idea what he was going to say to her, let alone how he could possibly convince her that her life was in grave danger—from Otto, her fiancé—and that he, Nicholas, had come to protect her.

Nicholas remembered her softness, her beauty, her trusting innocence. Her hair had been silken flame; her brown eyes as luminous and quiet as a fawn's. Just the memory brought a sense of hollow pain to his chest. There had been a time when he could have talked her into anything.

No. She wasn't that woman. Maybe she never had been. Now she thought she belonged to Otto.

Nicholas kept working silently, grimly, quickly, but without success. The metal blade kept clicking impotently. Anya's party would begin in less than an hour.

The blade jammed.

Damn. He didn't have the touch.

He managed to pry it loose. For hours, it seemed, the inane jokes went on beneath him as his blade strained inside the stubborn lock, as he agonized over how he was going to approach Evangeline, as the precious seconds ticked away one by one.

Then, just as he was about to give up, something in that hellish metal trap gave.

In his excitement, he dropped his tool. It clattered against the glass door as it fell. *Thowop!* It hit painted white aluminum.

Damn.

With a groan he knelt to pick it up. There was a sudden hush beneath him; the relaxed banter and jokes stopped. There was a new urgency in the Italian voices.

"*Dio!* What was that?"

Nicholas's hand froze in midair as he reached for the black-and-gold box.

"The balcony."

The men were shouting the alarm just as Nicholas opened the door and stepped silently into a gleaming cocoon of pink Carrara marble. His bad leg was throbbing, and his limp was more pronounced. The fragrance of a thousand roses filled the air. After the smoke, he felt slightly nauseated.

He saw gold vases filled with pink roses. A Titian hung on one wall; a magnificent Gobelin tapestry was on the other. Mirrored doors ran the length of the cabin. The nearest door was opened. He saw dresses hanging inside it. The last two doors were also slightly ajar. Filmy traceries of perfumed steam seeped out of them. A bathroom. The floors were covered with thick Persian carpets.

Nicholas felt repelled by Otto's extravagance. Otto hadn't changed. He had always used his money to overpower, to impress, to enslave and corrupt—to buy even those things in life that no man should ever have to buy.

In the center of the vast stateroom was a bed covered with a pink silk spread. Otto's bed. Hers, too. Nicholas flinched at the thought and then pushed it from his mind, concentrating instead on the black silk evening gown that lay there. The dress was lined with red taffeta. A heavy collar of diamonds and bloodred rubies had been tossed down beside it. Nicholas picked up the necklace and fingered it grimly. It was the kind of thing Anya wore. He pitched it back onto the bed.

It was clear as day that Eva was already Otto's mistress, that she was only too happy to be the newest piece of merchandise on Otto's auction block.

What was her price? A necklace of diamonds and rubies? No. More. Much more. On the bed beside the

necklace were catalogues of priceless illuminated man-
uscripts, and then Nicholas remembered she had a shop
to finance. Otto's money could give her success, her
family's respect, status in society, all the things a man
like himself could never provide.

Sour grapes, old man? Nicholas laughed mirthlessly
at himself. Who was he to judge her after the things
he'd done? Besides, it wasn't as if he wanted her for
himself.

Where the hell was she?

Restlessly he moved farther into the bedroom. On a
wing-backed chair he saw bits of fragile black lace. She
had always been messy. He picked one up, examining
what he discovered was a filmy brassiere. For a second
longer he let it dangle against his brown arm while he
imagined the creamy smooth swell of her breasts filling
it. Feeling aroused somehow, he flung the intimate
gossamer thing down again.

Damn Otto for forcing him into such a degrading
position. He had no wish to spy, no wish to sneak
around a woman's bedroom and invade her privacy,
especially not Evangeline's. Still, the picture of white
skin and dark nipples pushing beneath black lace lingered like an erotic dream in the back of his mind.

Nicholas heard the splash of water, the husky mur-
mur of a familiar French love song. The very song he
had once so lovingly taught her. He looked up and was
electrified when he focused on that cloud of steam sifting from that last half-opened door. A bar of pink-gold
light fell across the rugs.

Dear God! Just his rotten luck! She was bathing!

He should go and come back another time.

But he couldn't. There was no other time.

He moved closer to those half-opened doors, closer until he could see the flutter on cranberry tiles of her pink silk robe that lay discarded beside the marble tub. Closer until he could see her arm rise languidly from the soapy bubbles, until he could see the tantalizing curve of her naked back coated with sparkling bubbles, until he could see the damp tangle of red hair spilling in wild disarray from the confines of the towel down her long graceful neck. A pair of tortoiseshell glasses lay on the edge of the tub. She turned slightly, and the profile of a breast rose above a mountain of bubbles. She ran a thick Turkish washrag over it.

His heart began to pound violently. He told himself to move away. Instead his muscles turned to stone, and he stood there rigidly, staring at her with the awe of a raw schoolboy seeing his first woman. Her skin was golden and wet from her bath. Her voice was soft and husky as she sang that half-remembered love song, every faltering note cutting like the sharpest blade straight through to his heart. Once, long ago, on a drowsy summer afternoon, when she'd hardly been more than a girl, he had taught her that song of lost love. And afterward he had promised he would never leave her.

But he had.

She was French. And sensuous. She had loved him.

No, dear God. She had lied! How she had lied. She had wanted to remake him into some ideal man she could love. After his lonely childhood and lonely life, he had been so starved for love and for family himself, he had concocted a fantasy about her and hers. The Martins were proud. For a hundred years they'd occupied positions of power and privilege while his own family had bred gamblers and rogues. Raoul had secretly admired the Martins and longed to be one of them, and that had made their dislike hurt all the more.

The sweat on his brow was thick again. He felt a vague nostalgia, a terrible loneliness. And remorse. Why the hell should he feel remorse when she had been the one to show him she could never really love him.

She was nothing to him now! Nothing, but he couldn't just stand back and let her die—not even to save his own skin. Not even to destroy Otto.

She lifted her left hand lazily from the tub and blew the bubbles from her fingers. An immense diamond glittered in the soft pink light. She stopped singing and moved her hand so that she could admire the white stone as it flashed.

There was a new coldness in the pit of his stomach.

So, she had told Otto yes. Because of the money, the status and the fame, he supposed. Like everyone else neither she nor the Martins could see past the image Otto so carefully projected. Her shop was in trouble.

How in the hell was Nicholas going to convince Eva to jeopardize Connoisseurs and go into hiding with him? To convince her that Otto was a villain?

Someone began to pound on the pink door. Nicholas started, jumping clumsily back toward the balcony. So clumsily that his arm bumped against the wing-backed chair. The black box with the gold ribbons went flying toward the bathroom, landing right in front of the bathroom door. Nicholas swallowed hard. There was no way he could get it. No way she could come out and miss it.

Of all the abominable luck.

More pounding. *"Signorina!* It's Paolo!"

Otto's personal bodyguard. Nicholas held a special grudge against him. Half Italian, half Arab, Paolo was

the loathsome bastard who'd done Otto's dirty work in
Africa.

"*Signorina!*"

"I'm taking a bath."

"I have to check the stateroom. The guards, they hear
somebody on your balcony!"

She turned off the faucet. Her voice was impatient.
"All right. In a minute."

Nicholas could hear her stepping out of the tub. He
heard water gurgling down the drain. There was no time
to do anything except react on instinct. He dived toward the open closet door, squirming behind a dozen
hanging dresses. Just as he was about to pull the door
closed, he stepped on something soft that yowled and
sprang at him viciously. A set of thorny claws raked his
bad leg. Needle-sharp teeth bit into his ankle.

A cat! He would have gladly paid the price of a
thousand barrels of Nigerian crude to grab the squawl-
ing thing by the scruff of its neck and give it a fierce
shaking. At the very least he wanted to yowl as indig-
nantly as the cat had. He bit his lip instead.

"Victor, darling. Are you into trouble?"

Nicholas smothered his cry with the back of his hand,
pushed the door open a crack and gave the monster a
gentle kick. He saw a blur of black fur leap wildly toward the sliver of light. Thank God! He had the closet
to himself.

The devil sat down in front of the closet to lick his
tail.

"Victor...you look upset." Eva's voice was soft and
husky and warm as she came toward the closet.

Through the crack Nicholas could see her. She looked
alluringly soft in her pink silk robe, the roundness of
her breasts too apparent against the thin material. Her

glasses had fallen down to the tip of her nose. Her hair was a shower of coppery fire. She bent, and the robe gaped open, revealing too much slender leg. Her beautiful smile was radiant and adoring as she scooped the black devil into her arms. "Look what I found, sweetie."

Sweetie... Nicholas almost strangled.

She held the black-and-gold box up for the cat to inspect as if he had the wit to do so. Black paws began poking playfully at the gold ribbon as she carried him toward the door that Paolo was pounding on.

Put something else on, Nicholas wanted to yell, something that isn't so transparent and doesn't cling like a second skin.

She opened the door and smiled charmingly at the tanned brute with the moody sensual face.

The man was as dangerous as a cobra. Nicholas sucked in his breath with hatred. Skintight suede molded Paolo's lean body. He had the look of a killer—with those opaque, soulless eyes and the hard thin lips that rarely smiled. Why couldn't she see it?

She had never been clever about men.

Nicholas remembered the opaque eyes, the way the thin lips had curved again and again when he'd plunged his bayonet into Jones's inert body before kicking him into the ravine. Paolo was the hit man Otto had sent to Africa.

The enticing charm of Eva's smile toward this monster roused a dangerous, murderous fury in Nicholas.

"*Signorina*, I need to look—"

His eyes slid over her lush body with a predatory interest.

Damn the man. Nicholas could have gladly choked him to death with his bare hands.

Paolo broke off, swaggered restlessly to the balcony and looked out, his every movement slow, suggestive, dangerous, as if he were casing the room. He lifted curtains, looked under the bed, and she watched him, unafraid.

As always she was incapable of seeing through a man like Paolo.

"There's no one here, Paolo, I can promise you. And the prince is waiting. I need to get dressed."

That was the understatement of the year.

Paolo's eyes went over her. He combed his fingers through his black hair, shrugged, and decided she was right.

When he had gone, Nicholas sagged against the wall in relief.

Until he realized he was going to sneeze.

Cats! He was allergic to them!

Gently Eva set Victor and the mysterious gold-and-black box down on the bed. Then she switched on the radio. For a second it blared, so she didn't hear the two very loud sneezes in her closet. Then she turned the radio down, twisting knobs until she found a lovely Chopin nocturne.

She had to hurry; Otto was waiting. She'd stayed too long in her bath because she dreaded facing all of Anya's glamorous guests. She loosened the sash of her robe.

Victor was on the bed with the mysterious black box, and he was snatching and pulling, making a hopeless snarl of the gold ribbons. She studied the box. Curious, she picked it up and held it against her ear, shaking it lightly.

Someone had been here. Why hadn't she mentioned the box to Paolo?

She shook the box again.

Because whoever had come in hadn't bothered the diamond collar or her. Because she could never have gotten rid of Paolo if she had, and his strange eyes made her feel creepy. He didn't bathe often enough, and when he came too close she could smell sweat and leather and stale wine.

As she undid the gold ribbons, she draped the long lengths across Victor who rolled over, winding himself playfully in the glittering streamers.

Holding the box in her bandaged hand, she tore into the black paper, tossing the bits to Victor.

Inside was a gold velvet box.

A tiny vellum envelope fell out. Her name was a swirl of bold black letters. Even her middle name that no one knew. For a long moment she stared at it. Long ago that single letter from Raoul had come to her from Africa addressed in the same manner. The handwriting was identical.

A shiver traced down her spine.

Then she tore it open.

Inside was a single card and more of the same bold black scrawl. She read aloud the terse message in French.

"Once I promised to return to you on your birthday, *chère*."

It was unsigned.

Her lips quivered. *Chère*. Only one man had ever called her that. Only one man had ever made her such a promise.

Raoul.

But he was dead.

Who else? Who even knew that today was her birthday?

Her family—but they were in Louisiana, and they would never be so cruel.

Numbly her fingers lifted the lid of the box. Shimmering against black satin was a golden ring with an onyx stone set in its center.

Mon Dieu.

She was breathless, shocked.

The ring was the one that Raoul had given to her when they'd been so in love. When he'd left for Africa, she'd given it back to him—along with a gold chain so he could wear the ring around his neck.

Her heart stopped and then began to flutter chaotically. Raoul's thick gold chain was looped through the ring, but one link was broken as if the chain had been ripped violently from his neck.

She thought of Raoul lying helpless, dying. The vision came to her of some brutal hand reaching down toward that limp brown neck for the chain. She wanted to remember all the hatred she'd felt for Raoul. But all she could remember was the grief.

Through a mist of emotion Eva stared at the glittering bits of gold. The ring couldn't be hers! She didn't want it to be!

The ornate stateroom with its pink marble and Persian carpets and fine oil paintings blurred. Victor and his tangle of gold ribbons were forgotten. The sickening sweetness of the roses made her feel nauseated.

In a trance Eva lifted the ring from black velvet. She turned it over. With her fingertip she traced the familiar initials, Raoul's and hers, entertwined—E.M. and R.G.

She gave a broken cry.

Then she screamed.

Once.

Before she fainted.

For a second there was no sound other than a wildly romantic crescendo of piano notes. Chopin's *Minute Waltz.*

Then Paolo began banging against the door.

Her scream pierced through every cell in Nicholas's body. He had remained in the closet, trying to frame the exact words he would say to make her understand.

At her scream his heart seemed to explode in his chest.

He told himself to stay where he was until he got a grip on himself. He told himself that he hated her, that whatever pain she felt meant nothing.

But as she fell, he sprang from the closet, forgetting the danger to himself. Eva was lying on the floor—soft breasts, slender waist, long shapely legs—a provocative curl of voluptuous woman. The pink silk wrapper concealed very little. Her glasses had fallen to the carpet. She was lovely, fragile. And so small and feminine.

If she had been beautiful eight years ago, she was even more beautiful now. Her features were gentle and sweet. She had the high cheekbones of a Cherokee princess. Her hair was scintillatingly thick, golden red. Her slim figure was fuller and more opulently lush.

He had no real taste for the kind of women he saw now—scrawny women, cold women, women who could never touch his heart as once Eva had.

Eva was as still as death; her golden skin as white as snow. Her ring was clutched in her fingers.

With exquisite care Nicholas lifted her into his arms, cradled her tightly against him and smoothed the tangled curls back from her forehead. She was warm and damp from her bath, deliciously perfumed. She had the same sensuous, exciting body he remembered.

He ignored the familiar stirring in his loins and carried her to the bed and laid her down, smoothing her hair out on the pillow. Her eyes fluttered open, and she stared up at him. Nicholas thought he saw a glimmer of recognition, but she lowered her thick black lashes before he could be sure. Her whispery voice was so soft he could barely hear her. "You're a dream. A dream... I hate you, but why can't I forget you?"

Dear God. So, she was haunted by painful dreams, too.

She closed her eyes completely.

To shut him out.

He shook her, but she did not open them again.

"This is no dream, Eva. No dream. I've come back. To protect you. You mustn't be afraid. Not of me, *chère*, no."

"No, I don't want you to be real."

He couldn't blame her as he glanced around the lavish room. She wanted Otto and all that Otto could give her. But she didn't know what Otto was. Very carefully Nicholas lifted her into his arms. Somehow he had to get her out of here. But as he headed toward the door, he heard the thunder of footsteps outside in the hall.

Then the pink door was starting to splinter beneath Paolo's black-booted heel.

Nicholas was trapped.

"*Signorina?*"

Otto was shouting, too. "Here's the key you fool." Then in a softer voice that would sound evil only to Nicholas, he heard Otto say, *"Liebchen?"*

Nicholas barely had time to ease her ring onto her finger, to lay her gently back down onto the bed, and cover her completely from neck to ankle with pink silk. He grabbed the velvet box and its wrappings—not so easily done because he had to yank the golden ribbon away from the growling cat-devil—and then slipped outside onto the balcony.

They were gone now—Otto, Paolo, the doctor—having made a lengthy fuss over Eva.

She had lain in her bed like one in a trance, her red hair spread in a tangle of fire against her white pillow, a dazed expression on her face, not answering their questions.

They had pressed.

She had told them nothing.

Which was damned odd, but Nicholas was thankful nevertheless, even though he was furious at himself for bungling everything.

The doctor concluded that she was suffering from nerves, that she was overly excited about the suddenness of the engagement and the party. No one thought to search the stateroom or the balcony again.

There were guards everywhere. All Nicholas could do was wait until they left for the party. Even after she was alone in the room again, Nicholas was afraid to show himself. How could he convince her she had to go into hiding with him? How could they escape the heavily guarded yacht together? What if she screamed again and brought them all back to the stateroom? Nicholas was under no illusions about what would be his fate.

No, somehow at the party he would have to find a way
to approach Eva when she was not so carefully guarded.
With the comings and goings of the guests, it would be
easier to escape.

The curtains weren't quite shut. There was a crack.
From time to time Eva would walk in front of it, and
Nicholas could watch her twisting the black-and-gold
ring on her bandaged hand. She looked pale, confused, distraught.

Once as she studied the ring, he'd watched her silent
face. He saw her lips tremble and a tear well out of one
corner of her eye and spill down her flushed cheek before she raised her hand to brush it away.

What was she thinking, feeling? She had said she
hated him. What would she do when they met?

Slowly, as he watched the most tantalizing dress-tease
he'd ever seen, he realized all that he had lost. He saw
her naked, golden-limbed and lovely. He saw her in
black lace and sheer black hose. He watched her pin up
her hair. He remembered how she'd been—innocent at
first and then wild in his bed. And in spite of all that
had gone wrong, he wanted her.

He clenched his shaking hands into fists. In his
mind's eye, visions of blood and death in the desert, all
the dreadful memories of Otto's treachery rose up to
haunt him.

She was sleeping with his worst enemy. Nicholas
cared nothing for her. She was nothing but a pawn in a
dangerous game he was playing with a dangerous man.

Nicholas had Otto where he wanted him. Only this
woman stood in the way.

Nicholas was trapped on the balcony while she
dressed. He should have looked away. He should have
shut his eyes.

But he didn't. Instead he watched her dress, and the sight of her lighted a spark of desire that burned him to the core. He felt a madness to touch her, to know the warmth of her, to know her softness, to caress her until she burned with a madness equal to his own. Once he had been another man who had dreamed of having a real life, and she was the woman he had longed to share it with.

Just once he wanted to have her again, after the long barren years. And this treacherous need filled him with hatred because she had given herself to Otto.

Nicholas felt his stubborn, intractable will sliding away—the powerful force that had kept his mask in place all these years—and he was suddenly afraid. This woman was dangerous to him. She made him forget who he was, how he'd taught himself to live. Just the sight of her brought back the dreams.

If he wasn't careful, Otto would win after all.

Nicholas was afraid of her, afraid of even talking to her.

But he had no choice.

If he didn't get her away from Otto, she would die.

Four

Eva could not stop thinking of Raoul any more than she could forget the onyx ring on her finger. Had he come to her room? Her vision now seemed heart-stoppingly real.

But he was dead!

The horizon burst into white flame and her confused thoughts returned to the present. The heavy, rain-scented wind ruffled the harbor. The immense ciga-rette tender bobbed up and down in the dark waves at the stern of *La Dolca Vita*.

She hated boats and anything to do with boats—deep water, rain, electrical storms. The mere thought of jumping down into that wildly gyrating death trap filled her with dread. She had never forgotten the horror of nearly drowning.

Eva's sparkly black high-heeled shoe flailed for the last rung of the ladder. The sea breeze was whipping her gown, exposing too much leg to Paolo down below. The water splashed against the hulls; she felt salt spray against her ankle.

She gasped. If she misjudged, she would fall into the water, and her heavy gown would pull her under.

"Careful, *Liebchen!*" Otto commanded in a cool autocratic tone from above.

White-faced, she clung to the teak ladder. At last her toe found the bottom rung. Paolo's strong arms came around her waist, and he lifted her down into the tender. Otto jumped deftly after her. She grabbed the rail, and Paolo let her go and cast off.

It would soon be dusk. On the front edge of the black storm, Portofino was still jewel pink and gold—a paradise of sun and sea—all sparkle and shimmer beneath a hazy violet sky. On one hilltop Anya's villa was brilliantly lighted. Although Eva was disturbed by what had happened in Otto's cabin and frightened of the wind and water, she told herself she'd soon be up there, safe and sound on dry land.

Otto smiled reassuringly, but his smile lacked warmth. There was some new tension in him. He cupped her chin. It was all she could do to endure his cold, possessive fingers.

Otto had thick white hair, bushy black brows and fox-sharp blue eyes. Eva didn't like the way his bright, feral eyes seemed to read her every doubt.

He was shorter than she. Plump and tanned, he carried his extra thirty pounds well. He had a large head, powerful torso and an equally powerful will. He exuded power. He was the kind of man few people crossed. She remembered how furious he'd been when she'd told him a little while ago that she didn't want him to announce their engagement tonight after all.

Otto carefully honed his public image. The newspapers said he was the most eligible bachelor in Europe. Architectural magazines ran stories on his castles. Art magazines published articles about his collection. Her parents had been thrilled for her last night when she'd become engaged to him. They would be equally disappointed in her when they learned what she'd just done.

With a frown, Otto lifted Eva's left hand and studied the diamond he'd given her. He had promised her he would not make the announcement—but very reluctantly.

"You're still angry."

His face was dark and sullen. "Do you blame me? I'm used to getting any woman I want."

"I'm just not sure," she whispered. "Please..."

The powerful engine of the tender roared to life and she tried to pull her hand from his, but he wouldn't let her.

"You're still pale," Otto murmured, his penetrating blue eyes searching her face. "What upset you?"

"Nerves. I told you I'm afraid of boats."

His expression changed. He saw too much.

She turned away, her gaze fixing on a sleek black yacht moored only a few feet away. It hadn't been there earlier.

"The engagement," she began, "the party, deciding to come here at the last moment. Everything seems so hurried."

"You screamed. Why?"

She could not say: *I saw him.*

"An anxiety attack. I'm not used to parties like this, mingling with royalty."

She was looking at the black sloop. There was something mysterious about her. Eva read the bold curls of gold script on her stern. *Rogue Wave.* The yacht's lines were so graceful that she made Otto's many-decked, floating giantess with her air conditioners and stabilizers and helipad seem elaborate and top-heavy.

"Did your scream have anything to do with your wanting to postpone the announcement?"

"Don't be ridiculous," she said, not meeting his eyes.

"Nicholas Jones never showed up." There was a grim note in Otto's voice.

"Oh. I was so looking forward to meeting him."

"You will have to enjoy me instead." The grim note took on a bitter edge.

She was aware of a stealthy movement at a darkened window just above the waterline. There were no lights below on *Rogue Wave,* but Eva was almost sure that someone was watching them from the dark.

Shakily Eva twisted the slender gold-and-onyx ring on her right hand. Someone had come into her room and had returned the ring that she had given Raoul. She had fainted then, only to imagine him in her room.

What was going on? Who was Nicholas Jones? Had he left the ring? Had he really known Raoul? But Otto had told her Nicholas Jones hadn't come.

All she knew was that this afternoon when she'd found the ring she had realized she wasn't sure she could marry Otto. But she had to tread carefully. Connoisseurs was too dependent on Otto and his friends. Otto was egotistical. If she humiliated him, he would ruin her.

Otto brought her hand to his cool lips. Then he seized the controls of the boat and he became more arrogant than ever. He leaned back and steered with a single finger. The boat jetted recklessly across the harbor, careening past moored yachts and showering them with its rooster tail of white spray, sending a dangerous wake in all directions. Eva gripped the railings in true terror. The powerful rush of damp sea wind tore her hair loose from its pins, whipping it against her cheeks. By the time they roared up to Anya's private dock, one glance in a chrome mirror told her that she looked as wild as if she'd just stuck two fingers in an electric light socket.

Otto turned toward her, thrilled. "Well, *Liebchen*, what do you think of her?"

She was still terrified from the ride across dark water and now furious, too. "What do you think of my hair?"

He plucked a pin out of the red frizz and handed it to her. "I love it. You look wild—half-tamed."

Half a dozen of Otto's liveried men helped her ashore, onto the dock that led to the platform for the funicular that would carry them up the cliff to Anya's villa.

"Perfect for a part in a Tarzan film," she retorted.

"Perfect to be my future gypsy princess," he murmured. "You are the first woman who has ever denied me her bed this long."

That again. "We are not married."

"That is so rarely an obstacle." There was a predatory gleam in his eyes. "Besides, everyone believes we are lovers."

"I—I don't care." But she grew very still.

He touched the diamond necklace, lifting a single bloodred ruby. His plump fingertip was cold against her throat.

"When a man marries at fifty-eight . . ."

She licked her suddenly parched lips. "For the fourth time . . ."

"Such a man knows exactly what he wants."

"You sound like you're buying a Renoir."

"You are worth far more than a Renoir." He smiled but his voice was cold.

There was an answering coldness in her own heart. What was the matter with her? Why couldn't she just do the sensible thing and marry this man her family approved of? Why did it feel so wrong?

He took her hand firmly and led her toward the funicular. He stepped into the cramped metal cage himself. Eva glanced upward at the steep tumble of jagged rocks.

"There are no roads to the villas," Otto explained. "Mule trains still carry most heavy items to the villas. I was very lucky to convince the local committee to allow me to build this funicular."

The cliff seemed sheer and almost vertical in places. Usually she wasn't afraid of heights, but a strong wind was blowing.

Paolo was shutting the gate on them, sending them up alone.

"No." Otto commanded. "I want you to stay with Eva—everywhere, every moment—tonight."

A look passed between the two men, some silent order, given and received. Otto pushed open the gate. Paolo squeezed his great body in with them. Otto punched a red button, and the funicular shot jerkily upward on a series of grumbling metallic groans.

The ascent was steep and terrifying, so steep that Eva didn't dare look down. By the time they reached the villa, the sky was almost totally black except for a few diamond-bright stars and flashes of lightning.

Otto left her with Paolo, and Eva found a bathroom and repinned her hair. When she came out she wandered among Anya's guests out onto the palm-shaded terraces that clung to the vertical cliffs. White lights had been hung in the trees, and the swimming pool that had been chiseled into the rocky cliff was a dazzling aquamarine color. Flowers were everywhere.

There were dozens of beautiful women in designer gowns and jewels. The finest French champagne flowed as freely as the sparkling waves lapping against Anya's dock below. The softly scented breezes smelled of salt air and summer blossoms—geranium, gardenia and oleander. The moonlit evening was idyllic, and yet Eva couldn't relax.

There was a ring on her finger that she couldn't explain. The man she had given it to was dead. She could not stop asking herself who had returned it to her and why? The mere thought of it was enough to send a strange tremor through her.

Portofino had not changed in fifty years. Ever since she'd arrived, she had felt as if she'd lifted the curtain of time and walked back into the past.

Near the pool behind her a pair of lovers were embracing secretively.

"Nothing ever changes here except the shift of the sun in the sky."

Eva recognized the voice of Il Padrino, the local godfather. He was speaking to a dark-eyed starlet. "We read, we relax, we talk, we make love...." The girl giggled invitingly.

Eva drifted away, but his words lingered in her mind, arousing that aching, unwanted emptiness that usually haunted her only in dreams. Raoul seemed eerily near. She went into the house and admired Anya's magnificent antiques as well as the paintings on the walls, which were masterpieces. She was fascinated by two paintings. The first was of the phoenix, that great mythical bird fabled to live five hundred years, plunging itself into a wall of flame that would be its funeral pyre. The second painting was of the same subject, but in it the phoenix was rising from its own ashes. She looked up and saw that Paolo was watching her.

Bodyguards—their necessity seemed sinister somehow. She shivered. The rich were as trapped by their wealth as were the poor by their poverty.

She moved toward Otto and his guests. As always he was using every minute to promote his businesses.

Once he had told her, "Like you, *Liebchen,* I'm a shopkeeper at heart."

"You keep a big shop."

He had laughed.

The glitterati of a dozen countries were there tonight. All were vying for attention, competing to see and be seen by the right people. There was a vicious social hierarchy even among these kings and queens of society, and she felt out of it all. But such freedom would not be hers much longer—not if she married Otto.

Hours passed. Eva moved through the throngs of guests on Otto's arm, very aware that she and his necklace of diamonds and bloodred rubies were on display just like his fabulous paintings. The guests believed what Otto wanted them to believe—that he and she were lovers.

For so many years she had worked hard for this moment.

She was the envy of everyone.

Never had she felt more utterly alone.

If she married Otto, she would have approval, success, children. But what of love?

Otto's guests expressed their interest in Connoisseurs. She found herself trying to act like Otto—using this social occasion to promote her business, but what she secretly wanted was to feel cherished and to feel wild about the man who would be her husband. She told herself that Otto was older; he'd known too much hardness in his life to ever wear his heart on his sleeve.

Suddenly she and Otto were standing beside a gold-and-marble table piled with a mountain of gifts. He was telling everyone stories of his childhood, how he'd grown up in Paris, a refugee of the Nazis.

"I learned early that life was precarious, my friends. You must seize what you want—whether it is an empire, a moment or a woman." The thin aristocratic lips parted in one of his sly-fox smiles. He lifted Eva's left hand so that everyone could see the diamond he had given her.

There were gasps. Then applause.

He had not actually announced their marriage. And yet he had.

Eva felt betrayed. She tried to smile but she could not be that false. She felt like her face was cracking. Her entire body was trembling. The ornate room with its velvet sofas, tall mirrors and elaborate oil paintings seemed to spin in a sickening whirl.

She felt Otto's cold lips against her cheek. "You are pale, *Liebchen*," he whispered, pretending concern.

Pale with suppressed rage. She could see the looks of envy on many of the women's faces. Again she tried to smile, but she was too angry. *Later,* she told herself. *Later. You will deal with him later, firmly but with care.*

Otto reached for the nearest gift, the largest one of all. It was wrapped in black paper and tied with golden streamers.

Black and gold.

The same paper and ribbon as the gift she'd found in her stateroom.

She glanced down at the ring on her right hand. In an instant her fury toward Otto was forgotten. All the remaining color drained from her face. Her knees felt like rubber. Uncertainly she turned to Otto, touched his arm and held on to him for support. He smiled at her, pleased.

Otto ripped into the paper and pulled out a tiny vellum enveloped and handed it to her. Otto's nine aristocratic names were mocking swirls of bold black.

Eva felt the blood rush back into her face.

On the card inside was a single word. Revenge. It was signed Nicholas Jones.

Otto caught sight of the message and then this fierce gaze flashed around the room. He spoke to her hurriedly, but she didn't hear him. The roar in her ears was too deafening.

Nicholas Jones—he was here! He was the one who had come into her room earlier.

The crowd grew quiet as everyone waited for Otto to open the gift.

She looked up desperately. "I thought you said he wasn't coming," she whispered.

She was shocked at the change in Otto. He seemed smaller somehow, as if he had shrunk a whole size. His face was very white. His thin lips were pressed together to conceal their trembling.

Across the room a tall man moved deliberately, drawing her attention away from Otto. He was tall and dark and dressed in black. He stood in the shadows beneath the golden paintings of the phoenixes.

She froze.

This time she knew.

His back was to her, but something about him was achingly familiar. She studied the way his tuxedo fit him so perfectly, emphasizing his broad muscular shoulders yet not exaggerating them, tapering at his lean waist. He was talking to Anya. He made a gesture with his hand that was peculiarly French—*Cajun French*—and yet peculiarly his alone.

Eva felt the shock of recognition go through her whole body.

The man turned slowly. There was an iridescent ribbon of golden light in his ebony hair. He lighted a cigarette and carefully shook out the match. That gesture, too, was peculiarly his.

Behind him the golden feathers of the phoenix seemed on fire.

Raoul.

Mon Dieu.

He was alive.

The vision in her stateroom had been all too real. The treacherous, lying devil who'd murdered a hundred men in cold blood for money was very much alive and prospering by the look of him.

Some part of her had always known he'd survived.

And yet this man with the black hair and the deep dark eyes and the devastatingly beautiful masculine face wasn't *her* Raoul at all. He was of some newer, crueler vintage. There were deep lines around his mouth that added a harshness and a terrible coldness to his features.

This man was ruthless. She knew that he had come into her stateroom and left a gift, his deliberate intention—to tear her heart to pieces. He was a stranger, either reborn or disguised as the man she had once loved, a stranger who mesmerized her with a vital, furious, animal magnetism that Raoul had never possessed. She had loved Raoul; this man aroused some darker, deeper emotion.

She had never quite believed Otto. Never until now. She had always believed that if only Raoul had come home, they could have proved him innocent of Otto's accusations.

Nicholas Jones appeared capable of anything.

She wanted to run, but she couldn't move a muscle.

Otto hadn't seen him yet, but his hands were shaking as he opened a case of the finest imported French champagne. He lifted a bottle and held it up for the crowd to admire. He tried to smile, but his face was a mask.

Everybody clapped and smiled. Everybody except Otto and Eva and the dark uninvited guest across the room.

For the first time the man looked directly at Eva. His cynical gaze met hers, touched hers with its mocking fire, and she felt an incredible shock go through her again. He felt it, too. Then his tanned face hardened, his black eyes narrowed, first with disbelief and then with a fresh blaze of anger and contempt. He lifted his champagne glass toward Otto and her in a mock salute before he turned back to Anya.

His face purpling, Otto jammed the bottle into its cardboard cradle and thrust the magnificent gift aside. He had spotted the swarthy uninvited guest beside his daughter. Instantly he called Paolo to his side and spoke to him in low, rapid whispers. Seconds later Paolo moved through the crowd toward Anya, but when he reached her, Raoul had vanished.

Somehow Eva and Otto got through the next hour. Otto opened his gifts while she read the cards for him in a voice that shook almost as much as his hands did. From time to time her gaze flickered about the room, searching for but not finding Raoul. After all the presents had been opened, guests began to come up to Otto and congratulate him.

Eva waited until Otto was surrounded. Then she slipped out of the house and raced down the stone steps and footpaths, past the huge rock walls embroidered with geraniums and cascading clumps of bougainvillea, past the aquamarine pool, and lost herself in the hanging gardens that clung to the cliffs in tiers of imported palms, eucalyptus, mimosas, flowing fountains, artificial waterfalls, and pines. When she reached the far corner of the garden, she came to a high glass wall that served as a windscreen and a boundary wall as well. A narrow lap pool reflected the dark shapes of the trees and the starry sky. Anya's brilliantly lighted terracotta mansion was almost invisible, so steep were the cliffs and dense pines, but Eva could hear the music drifting down from the house.

Where was Raoul? Why had he come back tonight?

Beneath she could see the harbor, the sparkling water and the lightning in the distance; she could smell the salt tang of the sea as well as the fragrance of nectar from the summer flowers.

More than anything she wanted to be alone.

She heard a stealthy footstep on stone. Someone had followed her from the house, someone who was hidden by the trees.

"Who..." Her voice was light and breathless.

There was no answer. Frightened, she took a faltering step back. Then another. Again she called out, but again silence was her only answer. As the heel of her shoe caught the edge of a brick, too late, she remembered the pool.

She fell backward, floundering wildly to save herself. A million reflected stars rippled across the inky liquid surface. She cried out in frustration, sputtering, as the water slopped into her sparkly shoes, then up to her waist and over her head. When she managed to stand up, her hair and her gown were a dripping mess.

"Oh!" She was pushing the oozing mass of her collapsed hairdo out of her eyes when a tall figure moved in the shadows.

"Very nice," a deep sarcastic voice drawled from the trees. A match flared. "A hell of a lot nicer than the first time we met, when I had to jump in, too."

He stepped nearer the pool. In the tiny curl of golden flame she recognized the raven hair, his harsh profile, his unsmiling, yet ever-so beautiful mouth.

"You!" she spat.

Nicholas Jones lighted his cigarette and shook out the match. In his flawlessly cut tuxedo, he was as elegant as she was not. His broad-shouldered physique was more heavily sculpted with muscle than she remembered. From her embarrassing position in that shallow pool, he seemed a gigantic being looming out of the darkness. He moved toward her with a slight limp until he stood directly above the pool, staring down at her. His face gave nothing away. The hard features seemed cast in bronze.

She swallowed.

It wasn't his vile misdeeds that she remembered. No, it was all the youthful pain of loving him and losing him that came back to her, the years of loneliness, as well as the bitter disillusionment of knowing he could never be the man she'd wanted him to be.

He had meant so much to her. She had meant so little to him. Most of all she hated him for that.

Only his eyes moved. They were insolent and black as they roamed the length of her, passing over her eyes and her red hair, to linger at her swelling breasts, clearly revealed by the ruined silk.

"Well, don't just stand there!" she hissed. "Do something!"

"The mistake I made was pulling you out of the river in the first place." At her quick frown, he grimaced. She could see his white teeth in the faint light, and there was mockery in his eyes.

She could have gladly choked him. "Please," she whispered with pretended meekness.

He leaned down and took her wet hands in his warm dry ones. Even this most casual touching was different with him than with any other man. She let her body go limp as he started to pick her up, so he had to put all his strength into the effort. Then just as he was lifting her out, she suddenly hunched, put both feet against the side of the pool and kicked.

With delight she heard his startled male yelp as he fell, then his furious splashes behind her as she heaved herself out of the pool.

A hand closed around her ankle like a vise and he dragged her roughly across the bricks into the water . . . into his arms.

"Not so fast, *chère*," he whispered.

"You're hurting me," she screamed, trying to protect her injured wrist.

"That was a nasty little trick," he muttered, pulling her more tightly against himself.

"And exactly what you deserved."

The damp straps of her gown fell over her shoulders, and the bodice slipped revealingly. Her wet breasts were mashed into his chest. His hard thighs trapped her legs as she thrashed to free herself. Her every movement only made her more aware of him as a man. There was something erotic about the cool water and his hot skin. Something erotic about wet clinging clothes.

"Maybe you are exactly what I deserve...." He held her tightly. He ran a caressing hand beneath her delicate chin.

"Let me go!"

His hands and eyes inspected her closely. There was something predatory in his every gesture. His masculine scent touched her nostrils. Her body had begun to tremble beneath the pressure of his hands. Her breathing became harsh and rapid.

His voice came low, like an animal growl. "You shouldn't have pulled me in if you didn't want my company."

"Why did you come back—tonight?"

"You wouldn't believe me if I told you." His fingertip started to push one of her fallen straps back up.

"Try me."

A charged silence fell between them.

She felt his finger on the naked skin of her shoulder and jerked away as if from flame. He was watching her, his dark eyes taunting as if he were as conscious as she that all that separated their bodies was two layers of thin wet fabric.

"To save you, you little fool. Otto von Schönburg is the worst scoundrel you've ever picked."

"I would be a fool if I believed you. You never cared about saving anyone but yourself," she jeered.

"Someone must have taught you that. The day we met I saved your life, remember?" His words were no more than a warm whisper. "Otto, I'll bet."

"He told me what you did—in Africa."

There was a sudden bleak wasteland of pain in Nicholas's eyes. She saw it and didn't understand it. But she felt compassion for him, which was absurd.

"I'll just bet he did. And you always were ready to believe the worst about me. You were determined to re-make me into some wimpy paragon your grandmother could approve of, and when you couldn't..." He forced himself to stop. "What else did Otto teach you?" He ground out the words with rough malice. And then, before she could stop him, he caught her shoulders and pulled her closer. "What else?" he whispered. "That question has driven me mad."

With the back of his hand he traced the softness of her cheek, the length of her nose, the voluptuous full-ness of her lips, reading her every feature with the exquisite gentleness of a blind man starved for the sight of the woman he loved. "You're still a very beautiful woman. Did Otto enhance your skill in bed? Not that you weren't good..." His fingertip moved insolently down her throat, and she began to quiver from the mesmerizing warmth of his touch. "Because you were very good, *chère.*"

"No..." She tried to shrink away from him.

"You were unforgettably good, and unforgettably beautiful."

Eva closed her eyes a moment. He was deliberately, cruelly humiliating her.

"Underneath all that determination to be a perfect Martin, with a perfect life and a perfect man, there's a passionate, beautiful woman who wants to be free to

find herself. Maybe that's why I can't let him kill you,"
he said softly. "I want to save that woman."

"Kill?"

His statement was so unexpected, so completely far-
fetched, that for a moment Eva could only gape at him.
"Otto—kill me? That's crazy! You're the murderer."

Nicholas's grip tightened on her arms. That bleak
dark look was in his eyes again.

"And you believed him, *chère?*"

"He showed me all the newspapers."

"Before or after he took you to bed?" His low tone
was unspeakably cruel.

"You know so much. You figure it out."

"I already have."

"Fine. Just go. I was doing just fine before you
showed up."

"It's easy to see why you think so. He told you you're
going to be his princess. Your family probably ap-
proves. Do they know that you share his stateroom, his
bed?" He lifted the ruby-and-diamond necklace from
her throat. "He gave you this to wear around your neck
like a dog collar. It's plain as day he owns you. Otto von
Schönburg is a powerful, evil man. He can buy and sell
newspapers, governments, human beings. He betrayed
me, Eva. He had my men killed in Africa. He defamed
my name with his lies. Now if I don't stop him, he's
going to kill you, to get at me."

"I don't believe you."

"You never could believe in me."

She flinched. Maybe once she could have believed in
him—if he had come back, if *he* had trusted *her.* But
now he was a cruel stranger, whose dark cheek she
wanted very much to slap. Instead she balled her fingers tightly into her palms and turned away. She did not

know that their discussion—her rejection, her disdain, all these things—drove him past the point of madness.

He held her fast. ''You were mine before you were Otto's. I can't stop myself from wondering whether the real thing is as good as the memory.''

His long fingers curved painfully into the wet tangled mass of her hair, bringing her head back so that the creamy smooth length of her neck and shoulders was exposed to his insolent gaze.

''I should never have pulled you in,'' she whispered weakly. The comment seemed inane.

''So, you're just now figuring that out.''

His dark head moved lower, and she could feel his breath against her cheek.

''No...''

''Yes,'' he murmured. Then his mouth came down on hers.

He had kissed her before, but never like this. Never with such greedy demand. Never with such angry passion and contempt. There were years of pain and need in his hot, savage kiss. And even as she fought him, she felt something darkly alive, some treacherous alien thing deep inside her, quicken in flaming, welcoming response. Her skin became warm satin beneath his callused fingertips, her body pliant beneath his. She let her mouth open.

He groaned. His tongue plunged inside the warm, sweet wetness of her lips. ''Dear God...''

Their tongues mated; their mouths clung. She tasted pool water mixed with tobacco and rum, and that special flavor that was his alone. A bewildering tide of emotions made her ache for his physical embrace no matter how much she hated the man he had become.

"The real thing is damned good," he muttered hoarsely before he kissed her even harder than before.

"So you're alive," she whispered a long time later, after he'd torn his mouth from hers. She was running her hands through his damp shining hair, holding her cheek close to his, not letting him go, forgetting all the evil he had done, forgetting the lies he had just told her, not caring if only he would go on holding her in this dark time of fevered madness.

"Would you prefer me dead?" he demanded.

Weakly she shook her head. No matter what he'd done, she didn't want that. "All those years... you could have come back."

"Without making the real killer pay? With my name blackened? With everyone believing me a murderer? Could you have stood by me and borne that kind of scandal?"

Once she had thought... But what did it matter? The past was over. With good reason he had not believed in her then. There was nothing she could say to convince him now.

"There was nothing for me to come back to," he said grimly at last. "Besides, Otto would have killed me."

"But you did love me."

"It was a mistake. A dream. I woke up and found that I was a fool."

"So you can't forgive me the past, nor Otto," she whispered.

Nicholas was silent. His dark eyes grimly studied the sparkling necklace at her throat. "I was not blessed with a forgiving nature."

"I can't forgive you, either," she said wearily at last.

"I don't want your forgiveness, *chère*."

"Then?"

His fingers tightened at the back of her neck, and as he forced her face toward his again, the diamonds cut cruelly into her flesh.

"But I can't let him murder you the way he murdered my men."

Then his mouth grazed hers with hunger again. "And I still want this, too," he whispered, shoving the strap of her gown lower and then moving the material of her gown. He touched her breast. His hand felt slick and wet and warm against her. "Only this. Nothing more . . . ever again from you." His voice was as brittle as glass, and just as cold and loveless. But there was fire in him, too. Fire in the mouth that closed over her breast and suckled there until she was limp and breathless. "You were made for my kisses, but for mine alone."

At last she summoned the will to try to twist away, but he kissed her hard on the throat, on her mouth, possessively as if he were branding her with his kisses. A million liquid stars sparkled over the water like dancing diamonds. He pushed her against the side of the pool and pressed his hard body onto hers.

The water was icy, but he was hot, like fire. So hot he was melting her with his heat.

"Not here," he said at last, his voice harshly resonant with passion. "Not now."

With new horror she realized just how far she'd let things go.

"Never," she vowed, but she was shaking when he released her.

She felt his hands at the back of her neck roughly undoing the clasp of her necklace. He pocketed the necklace. Then he yanked off her clip earrings and her diamond ring.

"What are you doing?" she cried, furious again as he tossed the earrings and ring into his pocket, too.

He took her by the hand and pulled her out of the pool. "I came here to save you from Otto. Not to steal anything that is his. We've got to get out of here. Fast."

"No! Everyone will think I ran off with you."

"That's what always mattered—other people's opinions."

"No... but Connoisseurs— You don't know what Otto will do if I humiliate him like that."

"I have a hell of a lot better idea than you." With a single fingertip he made a swift slicing motion across the base of her slender white throat.

The mere gesture made her shake from the cold. She pulled her hand free of his and would have run back to the house. But he grabbed her and yanked her down the path that led to the docks beside the glimmering dark water of the harbor a thousand feet beneath.

"I don't have any clothes... and my contact lens stuff. And my cat! I can't leave Victor!"

"If I go after that cat, I *am* crazy!"

"Where are you taking me?" she whispered.

"Out there." He pointed at the lightning that burned the black sky with livid silver-white fire. "We're sailing straight out into the Med—into the teeth of that hell."

"That's suicide."

"That's why Otto won't follow us."

Eva tried to tear her hand away, but Nicholas gripped it tightly.

"You are crazy," she breathed.

His eyes were hard and dark and terrible. "I know."

"What about my cat?"

"Not that crazy, *chère!*"

But he was.

Five

Even the slight flutter of his swollen eyelids when he opened them caused waves of pain to pulse in Paolo's brain. His throat was raw. Through the blur of his own blood, he saw vivid red spatters all over the white-painted aluminum, and he knew that, too, was his own blood.

Dio.

His black suede pants were so damp with the stuff they stuck to his legs. The balcony looked like Girouard had mopped it with blood.

Paolo struggled heavily to his feet and shuddered convulsively. With a bloodied hand he pushed aside the pink curtains and stumbled back into the stateroom. Girouard had dragged him outside, nearly strangled him.

Except for the moonlight and the flashes of lightning, the room was dark. Still, he could see that Girouard had made a mess as he'd hastily packed. Signorina Martin's leather bag, most of her clothes, even her cat were gone.

Paolo had been waiting in the dark for him to come, and he would have gotten him if only he hadn't slipped on that damned cat.

Girouard had come from behind and struck him down.

A single piece of paper fluttered on the bed beside the dark glimmer of the woman's jewels.

Girouard was a fool for leaving the jewels and taking the woman. Paolo picked up the note and read the bold black scrawl.

There was a single word.

Revenge.

Girouard's taunt brought a fresh swell of bitterness into Paolo's heart, and he damned Girouard to the worst hell imaginable.

Paolo staggered to the balcony. What he saw made him utter a muted cry of rage. *Rouge Wave* was beating its way through the rough seas and high winds straight into the frothing violence of the Mediterranean.

No one deliberately left a safe harbor and sailed into a storm like that.

No one but a crazy desperate fool like Girouard.

Paolo crumpled the note into a bloody ball, struck a match and set the paper on fire, letting it burn down until he smelled the vile stench of his own flesh. Then he pitched the blackened fragments onto the priceless carpet.

Revenge would be his. Not Girouard's.

Girouard would pay dearly, and so would the woman.

Paolo imagined her slender white throat. He saw it covered with blood, and this vision made him swell with savage excitement and male power. He would make Girouard watch while he murdered her.

She would not be his first woman. But he would enjoy her more than most.

A cat's claw found its way through the soft leather bag and raked Nicholas's shoulder.

Damnation! Eva had been right. He was crazy. Crazy to go back to *La Dolce Vita*. Crazy to risk his neck for a cat.

Nicholas jammed his great bruised body into the doorway so he could brace himself against the yacht's bucking movements. He was holding the leather bag, struggling to unlock the door of the forepeak cabin where he had left Eva and dreading his reception all at the same time.

Outside the seas were streaked with foam; the gale-force winds were shearing the tops of the highest waves and pounding them onto *Rogue Wave*'s decks. Zak was at the helm, steering the boat so she would run with the storm. Nicholas had to get up there as soon as possible and shorten more sail. But first he had to deal with Eva. He had to find out if she had deliberately sent him to his probable death.

Nicholas threw the door open and saw her.

A single light glowed in the cabin. The room was tiny and plain after the magnificence of *La Dolce Vita*. The richly glowing teak walls smelled of teak oil—he had rubbed every layer into the wood himself. The brass fittings had been polished with equal tenderness and care.

Eva was exactly where he'd left her, still cowering on his bed in frozen terror, so wet and pitifully bedraggled, a different man in a different mood would have felt sympathy.

He remembered how close she'd once come to drowning, how terrified she'd been of boats and water afterward. She looked so fragile, so lost, that despite his foul mood, her appearance began to bother him. Her eyes didn't darken at the sight of him. Instead she looked relieved. Hers was not the face of a woman who'd sent a man to his death. But he couldn't weaken; he wouldn't weaken.

He tossed the black leather bag onto the bed. "Your cat, madam."

The boat heeled precariously, and the door slammed shut behind him.

"My—" She looked up, startled by Nicholas's cruel tone, by his stern expression.

A feline howl of outrage erupted from the bag.

"Why you beast!"

She wasn't referring to the cat.

"How could you? What kind of man are you that you would take pleasure in frightening a small, helpless animal?"

"That monster is about as helpless as a rabid sewer rat!"

She unzipped the bag carefully, and Victor clawed his way to freedom. He scrambled to the safety of the darkest corner and stared at them both with ferocious yellow eyes.

"What did he do to you, sweetie?" she whispered. Victor yowled plaintively back at her.

Nicholas felt an inane jealousy that she felt sympathy for the cat instead of for him. "A better question is what did he do to me? His claws are like ice picks. He sank every one of them into my hands when I put him in that bag. Then he scratched me again while I was carrying him here. I damned near died because of that cat."

If it hadn't been for the cat, Nicholas would have died for sure, but that was a bit of information he would keep to himself.

For the first time since Nicholas had come in, Eva seemed to forget her fear of the incessant pitching of the boat and the tremendous noise the yacht made slamming into the waves. Instead she concentrated on him. She looked at his hands that were crisscrossed with a dozen bloody scratches. At the purple bruise along his cheek.

"What happened to you?"

He had to fight his reaction to the concern in her eyes and to the slight quiver in her voice. She could be acting. He forced himself to move in for the kill. "You probably knew Paolo would be there waiting for me. Did you hope he would finish me off?"

With a gasp, she jerked back from him, letting go of the bunk railing. "No..."

The boat hovered on the top of an immense wave and then raced down it like a roller coaster car. She lost her balance and fell, tumbling across the bed, her head banging into the headboard. As she pulled herself up, he saw the faint trace of blood upon her lower lip. She touched her mouth, but said nothing. She merely looked at him with the hurt look of an abused child.

It was his fault she had fallen. His fault her lip was cut and bleeding.

He sank down beside her. Suddenly he felt terrible "Eva, I didn't mean it."

"Yes, you did. You are determined to be as mean and hateful as possible. Surely you must know I'm not such a horrible person that I would do a thing like that. No matter how furious I was at you, no matter how terrified."

"I know," he said quietly.

She took his battered hands in hers and gently touched the scratches one by one.

Her damp hair smelled of honeysuckle. Of home. Of all the beautiful things he had left behind, of the life he had once longed for, of all that was forever lost to him.

"You need to wash your hands. Cat scratches get infected easily."

"That figures. Everything about that cat is a nuisance."

Victor heard him and gave a faint yowl, almost as if he were defending himself.

Eva touched Nicholas's bruised cheek, and her fingertips were lightly caressing and deeply soothing. No other woman had hands like hers—long-fingered and slim that could either soothe or arouse. They smoothed the blood-soaked, wet tatters of his shirt. Gently she wiped the water that was streaming from his hair away from his brow, and though he willed himself to move away from her and the treacherous, warm pleasure of her satin touch, he couldn't. Her hand trembled just slightly above the blackest part of his bruise. "Oh, Raoul...Nicholas, I mean," she breathed. "It must have been a terrible fight."

"It was."

"Paolo—is he..."

Nicholas saw the look of horror in her beautiful eyes, and he grew angry all over again.

"No. Unfortunately there'll be no new . . . murder to further blacken my name," he jeered bitterly.

"You shouldn't joke about such things. Do you have a medicine chest?" Her voice grew softer still. "So I can clean these cuts."

His dark gaze met the gentle glow of her eyes. The hope for some happiness with him seemed to tremble in her tentative expression, and he felt drawn to her.

What was he doing? After all his resolutions to feel nothing for her?

Too well he knew the dangers of her gentleness and kindness. Ever since his mother had died when he was a baby, some secret part of him had longed for a woman's kindness, making him especially susceptible to it. Kindness was the one thing that could rob his soul of anger. For eight years he had lived on anger, on hatred, on revenge. Anger had driven him to make his own fortune and destroy his enemy's. He had forgotten how to live any other way, and he didn't want to learn.

"I'll do it myself," he said cuttingly, pulling his hand away from her.

She glanced down quickly to hide from him the fresh sparkle of tears in her golden-dark eyes. But he felt them. It was as if her pain was his.

God, why was there this bond between them? How could she still seem almost a part of himself? Why did she have to be so beautiful? What made him so vulnerable to her shimmering eyes, to her red hair and to her pale, translucent skin? To the velvet sound of her voice? It alone could arouse in him feelings of confused mutiny against every rule that he lived by.

Other women were as beautiful. She was a woman, like any other woman.

But she wasn't.

He clenched his hands to keep from reaching out and drawing her into his arms. He could understand the desire he felt for her, but he could not understand why she alone could arouse all these other complex feelings.

Because of him her graceful figure was coiled into a frightened, vulnerable ball. Because of him her eyes were downcast and her pale fingers were tensed. He had always been able to hurt her too easily.

He remembered the first day he had pulled her lifeless body from the river. With his own breath, he had given her life. She had been a child gently raised, he a man with years of hard living behind him. He had been a Girouard, she a Martin, and their families had disliked each other for a hundred years. But from that first moment when he'd held her in his arms and prayed with all his heart for her to live, it had seemed she belonged to him.

He drew a shaky breath and got up. His cabin seemed suddenly too small for the two of them and much too intimate a thing to share.

In those brief two years when he'd loved her, when he'd waited for her to graduate from college, she'd shown him a softer side of life and made him see beauty in things and people and in nature. She'd loved as easily as he'd hated. But that golden time had been obliterated by Africa and Otto's betrayal, by the knowledge that such a woman could never really love him when his name was blackened with the foul stench of murder, and his heart blackened with the lust for revenge. He wanted no more softness, no more beauty—they only made the hard realities of his life more unbearable.

"Where will I stay?" she asked.

"In here. With me."

"There's no way I can share a room with you," she whispered.

"Do you think I want you to?" The hoarseness in his low tone betrayed him. "It was me or Zak." Not even to himself would he have admitted he would have killed any man who tried to sleep with her in his presence. "I drew the short straw."

She said nothing, but he saw a single tear slip down her flushed cheek. She looked young, lovely and infinitely sad.

Sheer strength of will was the only thing that enabled Nicholas to stand up, to move away from her instead of to her.

Rogue Wave fell sideways off a wave. The cabin light dimmed into total darkness. Pillows, charts and a flashlight tumbled from the shelves, and she screamed. The light flickered back on, and he saw the stark white terror in her face. Nicholas had to take the wheel and fast.

The only comfort he offered was to ignore the incident as if it were nothing to cause alarm. He moved to a locker.

"Paolo will tell Otto I took you. They will come after us."

"Then everyone will think I ran off with you?"

"I suppose they will," he said indifferently, rustling through the messy locker, his main concern *Rogue Wave*'s lousy performance. Zak was a great navigator, but as a helmsman he lacked something. The yacht was being beaten to pieces.

"Connoisseurs...my independence...are all gone because of you. You ruined my life once before. Now you're doing it again."

"Would you rather die?" He pulled out a shirt. "If your shop gets into trouble, get your rich father to bail you out. He's done it before. And more times than either of us can count."

"How can you, who prize your independence so much, say that to me?"

"I'm a man," he replied curtly.

It was going to be a long night, and Nicholas was wet to the skin. He stripped out of his wet shirt, and that was a mistake, too.

Not only terrified, but now furious, too, she was up on her haunches, watching him. When she saw the scars on his back, her expression changed again, and the deep concern he saw in her eyes made his hands unsteady as he pulled on his dry shirt.

"What happened to your back?" Her words were muttered shudderingly.

He turned away from her and yanked his foul-weather jacket on, pulled the hood over his head and snapped a dozen snaps.

"It was a long time ago."

"In Africa?"

"Yes, damn it."

"You were beaten." A spasm of pain passed across her beautiful face. "Brutally beaten."

"Like I said, it was a long time ago." His voice was angry and gruff. "I lived through it."

"Did you? Or did the scars go so deep they twisted the inside of you as badly as those outside lumps of flesh?"

"Damn it! If you don't like the way I look, don't look at me then."

Her gaze moved over his broad shoulders, his muscled back, his lean hips. "I didn't say I didn't like it."

Something in her soft tone made him forget the boat, made him forget the storm—made him forget everything else but her. He could feel the beat of his heart pulsing in his fingertips, in his throat.

His gaze slid over her. He could see the shape of her breasts beneath damp, clinging silk.

He made his voice as hard and cold as granite. "You need to get dressed yourself before you catch your death in those wet clothes." The leather bag lay between them on the bed. To vent his frustration he grabbed the bag, turned it upside down and started ripping clothes out.

A black bra got caught on his scratched hand. He shook it loose, but not before he felt the hot blood creeping up over his cheeks.

He was blushing! Like a high school teenager! Thank God for the dim light.

But she saw. "Are you going to watch me?" she whispered.

Nicholas grimaced and wondered if she suspected he'd done so before. "If you're smart, you won't play with fire."

"If you were smart, you wouldn't have brought me on board."

"Well, it looks like we're stuck with each other," he muttered. "For better or worse."

"That sounds too much like a marriage vow."

Suddenly a huge wave picked the boat up and rolled it on its side. Nicholas's great body was flung across the bed, on top of her.

For one long hideous moment, the boat stayed there. His arms and legs were intimately splayed across hers as they slid together down the width of the bed. He felt her breasts, her tiny waist, her long legs tangling around his. Under different circumstances he might have been tempted, but he heard water gushing inside the hull somewhere. If they took another knockdown before they could pump out the bilge, they could sink.

"I've got to get up on deck," he muttered brusquely, scrambling to free himself of her.

She clung to him and buried her face in the hollow of his neck, terrified. "Don't go out there."

He held her close as the boat slowly righted itself. Then he loosened her cold, clinging hands. "Stay below." When he saw that her eyes were still wide with fear, his voice gentled. "Hey, there. I'm not going to let anything happen to you."

"It's not me I'm worried about." There was a hush. "It's you."

He tore his gaze from her ravaged face. That was something he couldn't, he wouldn't accept.

Carefully he eased her back onto the bed. "Try to get some rest."

It seemed as if he'd been gone for hours. The reality was less than ten minutes. At first Eva had been cold and shivering in her wet silk gown, with her soaked hair. Now she lay in a pool of grit and sweat. The air in the cabin was dank, the salt from the sea air permeating everything. The cotton sheet was as rough as sandpaper against her hot skin.

Rest! Was he insane? To sleep down below as the boat pounded through the waves? As a little girl, she'd always thrown up after carnival rides. This was worse, infinitely worse, because the ride went on and on. The constant motion of the boat flung about everything that was loose. She was bruised all over from sliding and falling. As she struggled to hold on, she envied Victor his claws that were sunk deeply into the upholstery of the cushions.

Soon she was so nauseated she couldn't even feel anger toward Nicholas for inflicting this torture on her. She was too ill even to care about Otto or Connoisseurs. Those concerns seemed to belong to another world. All she cared about now was the boat and Nicholas, and despite his abysmal behavior, she was very worried about him on deck, risking his life, struggling to sail the boat and keep her safe.

Eva lay as still as was possible, and finally she felt slightly stronger. With Nicholas at the helm, the boat did seem to move more smoothly. She decided to change out of her wet clothes and brush her hair, but when she tried to stand up, she felt sick all over again. The boat was rocking so forcefully it was difficult to do even the simplest thing.

Somehow she managed to undress and pull on jeans and a shirt. Never before had she realized what a land creature she was. Fervently she longed to be back on dry land, to stand upright, to lie in a bed that did not move.

Every time the boat rode a wave to its crest, it hovered at the top before careening over it and slamming down into the trough with tornadic speed. Eva had heard of boats breaking up at sea, of sailors being washed overboard. What was happening to Nicholas, who was out there exposed?

Lightning crackled outside, and she stared out a porthole and saw a brilliantly lighted, rain and wind-scoured sky. *Rogue Wave* had tall aluminum masts. Where did lightning go when it hit a sail boat? What would happen to Nicholas if the boat took a direct hit?

She hadn't wanted to share this cabin with him, but not sharing it was worse. He exuded self-confidence.

Even his deliberate insults distracted her so that she didn't worry quite so much about everything else.

The static blast of a radio in the main cabin made her jump. She heard the deep timbre of a man's voice. Hoping it might be Nicholas, she cracked the door. Instead she saw a tall black man with dark eyes and golden skin. He wore a T-shirt and white jeans, and he was huddled tensely over the radio. He looked up briefly and nodded toward her when she came in, but kept talking into the mike.

So this was Zak. He looked every bit as tough and hard as Nicholas.

"*Highlander Beauty,* we make our position to be..."

He spoke in a beautiful British accent.

Holding on to the walls, Eva made her way into the main cabin. She listened to every word Zak said, and watched everything he did. If only she could figure out how to operate the radio, she might be able to get a message out. The boat lurched wildly. Charts, gear, antennae, books and plastic containers flew off the shelves.

Zak seemed to take it all in stride as he answered another distress call on the radio.

"There's a lot of traffic in the Mediterranean. It's dangerous in any kind of weather at night, but in a storm it's even more so," he said after he finished the call.

Ships! They might be hit by a ship! Why hadn't she thought of that? She began imagining ships creeping up from all directions. A ship could crush *Rogue Wave* like a matchbox.

Again and again Zak used the radio, sometimes to answer a call, sometimes to make one. Every time he did, she watched him and listened intently.

GET 4 BOOKS

Return this card, and we'll send you 4 brand-new Silhouette Desire® novels, absolutely FREE! We'll even pay the postage both ways!

We're making you this offer to introduce you to the benefits of the Silhouette Reader Service™ : free home delivery of brand-new romance novels, months before they're available in stores, AND at a saving of 28¢ apiece compared to the cover price!

Accepting these 4 free books places you under no obligation to buy. You may cancel at any time, even just after receiving your free shipment. If you do not cancel, every month, we'll send 6 more Silhouette Desire novels and bill you just $2.47* apiece—that's all!

Yes, please send me my 4 free Silhouette Desire novels, as explained above.

Name

Address   Apt.

City   State   ZIP

225 CIS ACJS

DETACH ALONG DOTTED LINE AND MAIL TODAY! – DETACH ALONG DOTTED LINE AND MAIL TODAY! – DETACH ALONG DOTTED LINE AND MAIL TODAY!

Get 4 Books FREE

SEE BACK OF CARD FOR DETAILS

DETACH ALONG DOTTED LINE AND MAIL TODAY! – DETACH ALONG DOTTED LINE AND MAIL TODAY! – DETACH ALONG DOTTED LINE AND MAIL TODAY!

FREE MYSTERY GIFT

We will be happy to send you a free bonus gift along with your free books! To request it, please check here and mail this reply card promptly!

Thank you!

BUSINESS REPLY CARD

FIRST CLASS MAIL   PERMIT NO. 717   BUFFALO, NY

POSTAGE WILL BE PAID BY ADDRESSEE

SILHOUETTE READER SERVICE
3010 WALDEN AVE
P O BOX 1867
BUFFALO NY 14240-9952

NO POSTAGE
NECESSARY
IF MAILED
IN THE
UNITED STATES

During a lull, after making them cups of hot tea, Zak confided to her that he liked rough passages. As she set her cup in the sink where it couldn't roll, she sank queasily down beside him with the knowledge she was definitely in the wrong crowd.

The wind screamed outside, louder than before.

"Here we go. We're in for another squall," Zak warned her.

No sooner had he said it than a gigantic wave smashed into the boat, knocking her down, this blow a worse one than when Nicholas had fallen on top of her. Zak grabbed her and held her tightly. *Rogue Wave* lay on her side, sliding down the wave as still another crashed over her. Everything that wasn't a part of the boat came loose—tools, teacups, the coffeepot. Water was spilling into the cabin through dozens of tiny cracks, near the windows, the hatches.

Mon dieu. Were they going to die?

"If she goes over, we lose our rigging, and our skipper," Zak whispered, his voice like death.

Nicholas... As the boat hung there with the waves pounding over her hull, Eva's heart filled with a wild, mindless terror.

What was happening to Nicholas?

Slowly *Rogue Wave* righted herself.

The latch on the galley locker had come undone, and the door was banging. Cushions, pieces of the stove, life preservers, as well as other debris were floating on the floor. But Eva didn't care. She crawled over the mess toward the aft hatch. She had to know if Nicholas had been swept overboard. Before Zak could stop her, she flung the hatch open.

Rain poured inside, drenching everything, flooding into the bilges.

"Eva!"

Both men shouted at her to go back inside.

Her only thought was for Nicholas. He was alive! Her only desire was to be in his arms. She started to climb out.

"You don't have a safety harness or foul-weather gear!" Nicholas shouted. "Go back inside!"

Zak grabbed her, but she shook him loose and climbed out into the howling fury of the storm. She was immediately in another world, a world of black mountainous waves, a world that was brutal and overpoweringly destructive. The wet wind tore her hair back from her face as she crawled on bleeding knees toward Nicholas, clinging to the lifelines, clinging to the sheets, the winches, the railings, dragging herself when she could no longer crawl.

Nicholas watched her, his dark face white with terror.

"Go back! Dear God, go back!"

Suddenly she looked past him and saw what he saw— a wall of black water so immense that she knew *Rogue Wave* could never survive it. Eva would never reach Nicholas before the wave crashed over them. Without a safety harness, she would be swept overboard.

All of a sudden he was shouting at her, encouraging her. "Come to me, *chère*. You can make it."

But she was too paralyzed with fear to move.

The towering wave seemed to hang there. In reality it was rushing toward her with the power of a freight train screaming down a track at top speed. Within seconds it would smash her to pieces.

In that last desperate moment Nicholas lunged for her. His hard arms and hands were like steel holding her safely aboard while the great wave broke over them, flooding torrents and torrents of salt water over them until the decks and the cockpit were awash and the water swirled to their waists.

He was holding the wheel, holding her, too. She clung to him, wondering if they would live or die.

Against the hurricane roar of the wind and the waves, her scream seemed no louder than a whisper. "Are we going to die?"

"No."

She felt his incredible strength, the incredible force of his will. He was life—*her* life. With all her heart she believed his power was more than a match for the fury of the storm. She was slim and weak, but it didn't matter as long as she was in his arms.

The boat heeled dangerously. Water was pouring through the open hatch into the cabin. Zak was yelling and cursing and pumping madly down below.

In that endless black moment when *Rogue Wave* hung to the outer limits of a watery death and disaster, Nicholas stared into her eyes with a fierce intensity. All hatred, all desire for revenge were gone. They were no longer two separate people with two separate hearts and souls, no longer at odds, but together; they were one. He was inside her, and he *was* her. The terror of knowing they would either live together or die together was both exquisite pain and exquisite pleasure. She clung to him, consumed by the heat of his will to love her and to save her.

Even as she watched him in wonder, *Rogue Wave* slowly began to right herself and glide down the remnants of the shattered wave.

They were safe, and still Eva could not hold Nicholas close enough. The coiled sheets had come undone and were in tangles. A spar was broken, but they were safe.

She wanted to weep with joy, to cling to him forever, but he had regained control of whatever emotion he felt in the aftermath.

They were alive! But there was no joy in his face. Only a new and terrible hardness.

"Don't ever do that again!"

It took Eva's shocked brain a second to interpret the harsh bite in his voice and to realize that he was furiously angry.

"I—I came up to see if you were all right."

"You little fool, do you think that's any excuse? What could you have done if I wasn't? That wave would have swept you overboard."

"I'm surprised you even care."

A muscle jumped convulsively at the corner of his mouth. His lips were clamped together in a thin white line. "You could have jeopardized the boat." His tone was grim. "Get below and help Zak pump. Now!" The last word was like the blast from a cannon.

She stumbled through the companionway into water that was ankle deep. The life preservers and cushions were floating; the charts that had fallen to the floor were sodden pieces of garbage. There was the faint, almost undetectable, smell of chlorine gas.

His ebony face tight with tension, Zak jammed the hatch closed behind her. "It's like trying to bail a lake."

He resumed pumping with quick, deft strokes.

She stared at the ankle-deep water, the ruin and mess. The enormity of what she had done hit her full force. Numbly she put her hand beside his and lent her strength to his. A long time later, when every muscle in her back and arms ached with exhaustion, she whispered, "Nicholas is furious."

"With good reason."

This truthful remark, uttered without a trace of animosity, only made her feel worse.

Ten minutes later during another lull, Nicholas came down and Zak took the helm. Nicholas was sopping wet and haggard with cold and fatigue, but he gave her a quelling look. She wanted to apologize, yet she didn't dare do anything but keep pumping.

He went wearily to the stove and lit it. Soon the smell of fresh coffee mingled with the dank smell of the cabin. Her stomach quivered uneasily, and she clutched the side of the boat for support until she felt a little better.

He ignored her, sipping his coffee, savoring the hot warm liquid until, at last, his brooding silence drove her to despair.

"Well, aren't you going to say anything?"

His tired face turned in her direction. "All right, then, I'll say something. What you did was damned stupid. I didn't bring you on this joyride to get you and everyone else killed.

She forced herself to look at him.

"I—I'm sorry."

"From now on you'll do exactly as I say. If we're to get out of this alive, we have to work together, not against each other. You're going to have to help me."

"But what can I do?"

"You can cook, can't you?"

It didn't seem a very good time to tell him that she couldn't, so she nodded weakly.

"Hot drinks and hot food are very reviving in a storm when you're wet and cold. Come over here, and I'll show you how the stove works."

She stood beside him and watched as he lighted and extinguished the propane stove, which remained level because of gimbals.

She tried to concentrate as he explained Zak's and his "passage" routines, but the boat rocked continually. She began to feel seasick again.

"During storms I usually take six-hour watches and Zak three-hour watches. He does the navigation, engine and systems maintenance and repair. Usually he cooks. But with you aboard, he can stand longer watches. You can keep us going."

She was feeling sicker and sicker. His dark face swam in a queasy whirl. "I—I think I'm going to be..." Her voice was a curiously empty sound, trailing away.

The cabin reeked of teak oil, chlorine gas and stale salt water.

"Ooo." She put a frantic hand over her mouth to warn him.

That motion and her pale distraught face must have communicated her need, because he slid an arm around her to steady her, his face grave with concern. "What's the matter."

"I—I think I'm going to be sick."

Very quickly he lifted her toward the sink and stood behind her, supporting her while she shuddered into the aluminum basin. Afterward, deeply ashamed, she wanted to cringe away from him.

"You were very...kind to help me," she whispered, hating the hot tears threatening to fill her eyes.

"Nonsense," he said gruffly as he reached past her and pumped cool fresh water from the reserve tanks into the sink and cleaned it. Then he poured her a glass of fresh water.

Even though the water tasted faintly of plastic, she drank deeply until he advised: "Just a little."

Then he led her to his cabin and helped her down onto the bed. When she was settled, he left her, and she thought he was done with her.

He returned almost immediately. "Close your eyes, Eva, and I'll wash your face."

She was too weak to resist. He had brought a rag, and he stroked her hot skin gently with cool, wet, soothing cotton, dampening her brow, her dry lips, her throat. Then he dried her face off with a fresh towel.

He was about to leave. "Oh, I almost forgot—" He pulled out a tiny, pink, circular adhesive.

"What's that?"

"A patch to put behind your ear. Zak uses them to prevent seasickness."

"You're a little late."

"Better late than never."

Her eyes met the tender, luminous darkness of his. "Yes..."

He was talking about patches for seasickness. She was gazing at him, at the way his heavy dark hair fell across his forehead, at the way his harsh-featured face was soft now as he tended her, and she was thinking along very different lines. He had held her so fiercely outside when the wave had crashed over them. Then she'd been almost sure that he felt something beyond passion, something that was deep and eternal, something he could share only with her.

She lay breathlessly still while he fastened the patch behind her ear.

Her eyes closed, she enjoyed the feel of his callused fingertips against her neck, behind her ear. Gently he smoothed the tangled red curls back from her forehead. He readjusted the bandage at her wrist.

In spite of everything, there was something almost pleasant about being sick. He was being so kind.

With her eyes shut, she could almost imagine that he was always so tender in his regard for her. In that moment she wanted nothing more than for him to stay with her through this wild violent night. Then she wouldn't mind being sick. She wouldn't even mind that he had stormed back into her life and ruined everything. She wouldn't even mind being on a boat so much.

But when she opened her eyes to beg him to stay, she discovered that he had already gone.

Six

The dark gray dawn was massing with purple clouds when Nicholas dragged himself wearily to his cabin. He was icy and wet, and his bad leg burned where the bullet had ripped into his flesh all those years ago. Despite his pain, his overwhelming sense of fatigue and his knowledge that they were still in grave danger, when he opened the door, nothing existed but the beguiling curl of slender woman beneath the rough cotton sheets in his bed.

The joy he felt at the sight of her came as a shock. She'd almost gotten them all killed, and yet, ironically, it was that very action that had diminished his anger toward her. On deck in the midst of that howling fury, with her in his arms, he had seen something, felt something, in her and in himself, something incredibly powerful, and he was at a loss to explain it.

His disturbing thoughts dissolved, not due to exhaustion, but the sight of her.

It should have been a warning.

The sheet was thrown off. Her bare arms hugged his pillow tightly against her abdomen. Her red hair was spread in a pool of flame over her own pillow. Her thin T-shirt and tight jeans, unclasped at the waist for comfort, revealed the lush curves of her body. No longer did she look ill. Instead she seemed to be resting peacefully.

The picture was perfect until his gaze fastened upon a very contented black fur ball nestled against her hip. Pointed black ears cocked toward him. Yellow eyes slitted, observed him.

Nicholas felt a swift surge of jealous dislike, but since it erased the annoyance of those softer, maudlin emotions threatening to swamp him, allergic or not, he was almost glad the devil was there.

That cat kept coming in handy in the damnedest ways.

Not that Nicholas felt an ounce of gratitude nor the slightest intention of allowing that fleabag to remain where he was—in his bed.

Silently Nicholas began to strip in the darkness. He pulled on a dry shirt and briefs. Then he leaned down, caught Victor under the belly and scooped him onto the floor. The thud of four cat paws on teak made the most satisfying sound. There. He had shown the devil who the boss was.

The mattress dipped as he slid his icy body in beside Eva. He turned out the light, and the cabin melted into darkness. He stretched out his lean frame beside her, every muscle aching with cold and exhaustion, his old wound hurting more than the rest of him put together.

He had thought he could more easily ignore her in the darkness, but he was wrong. He caught the sweet delicate scent of honeysuckle. Another faint aroma drifted indistinctly to his nostrils. Her scent. The earthy, delectable scent of his woman. It was an elusive essence, but it made him remember long, hot, Louisiana nights when the air had smelled of damp earth, crepe myrtle and magnolia blossoms, of honeysuckle and wisteria. He'd lain with her, and they'd made love in the slanting, silver-white moonlight.

He remembered too clearly the way her mouth was soft and sweetly giving against his, the way her body had fit his perfectly, and the familiar memories stimulated masculine reflexes despite his aching exhaustion. She tempted him as no other woman could. She was French. A part of everything that he had been bred to. Dear God...

The warmth from her body seeped toward him beneath the sheets, and it took all his strength of will to cling to the hard wooden edge of the bunk and remain as far from her as possible. Adrenaline and other hormones—male ones, all of them, he was sure—pumped through his nervous system. His fingers knotted in an iron grip around the teak railing.

She exhaled softly, her breathing gentle. She was as undisturbed by his presence as he was violently disturbed by hers. He lay there, shivering and wretched, but with fiery desire torturing every cell in his body. *Rogue Wave* fought her way through the heavy seas, but he thought only of the woman beside him who seemed to breathe more gently, to sleep more easily now that he was near.

Surely this wild night was the design of the devil himself—first the storm, the long hours at the helm with blasts of black wind, waves and rain, and now to have to lie beside the one woman he wanted more than any other. He knew, though, that to take her would only make him all the more vulnerable to her.

He heard his own breath coming quick and harsh, and the sound of it shook him. He wanted her with an intensity that truly frightened him.

He did not know that she was awake, too; that she was as aware of his presence as he was of hers.

At last sleep came to them both. He dozed fitfully at first, as if all his muscles and nerves were wound tightly with tension. Then slowly a warmth stole through him, relaxing him, easing his exhaustion as well as the throbbing pain in his leg until he slept as carelessly as a child.

He awakened and was startled to discover the reason for the soundness of his sleep. She was beside him, her warm, satin-soft body cuddling against him trustingly, the perfumed waves of her honeysuckle-scented hair spreading over his chest and arms, her long jean-clad legs tangled deliciously in his.

She stirred in his arms, and without thinking he brushed his lips into her hair, against her throat. He felt her pulse race in response beneath his mouth. He stroked her breast, wanting more of her. All of her. Even as his hand drifted from her breasts to her belly where her jeans were unfastened, even as it slid inside to caress the bare flesh of her stomach, he told himself to stop. He had no right to touch her, nothing to offer her but more pain. Besides, to do so was to inflict the most exquisite form of torture on himself. With a groan, he rolled away from her to a spot where he lay shaking all over.

For a long moment he felt that he had to take her, that he had pushed himself too far this time, that he would die if he didn't have her. Then, with a supreme effort of will, he forced himself to remember Otto and Paolo, who would try to hunt them down and kill them as soon as the storm lessened. He remembered Paolo's stench of sweat and leather, his fist slamming against his jaw and pounding into his stomach in the stateroom. If it hadn't been for that cat and that blind, lucky blow into Paolo's thorax, Nicholas might be dead already because of her. Eva was dangerous, in too many ways to count.

Nicholas got out of bed and sank to the floor. The boat was pounding into the waves, but the teak felt cool against his feverish skin. He remembered Africa, the coldly savage murders of his men, and his own fierce need to gain revenge. Gradually he began to calm down sexually.

A velvet paw touched his hand. Then Victor curled up beside him. The cat did nothing else, and Nicholas pretended to ignore him. Since there was no one to see, he let him stay. They sat together, male to male, in silent camaraderie. After a long time Nicholas remembered he was allergic to cats, and he sneezed. But the beast seemed so settled, he let him stay anyway.

It was close to noon on that dark gray morning. One minute she was cosily nestled in warm sheets dreaming that she lay in Nicholas's hard arms. The next minute she was yanked brutally awake by hard arms that ripped the sheet from her body.

Nicholas looked bright and alert, as if he'd been awake for hours.

"Galley slave," he said provokingly, "get up. It's time you earned your keep! You damned sure weren't much use last night after you got sick!"

Her eyes snapped open. There he was, gypsy dark, his wolfish black eyes agleam as he loomed over her, rousing her in the worst possible way a woman could be awakened.

Forgotten was the tender lover of her dreams. Forgotten, too, was her fierce protector in the storm and the nurse who'd gently tended her.

"Get up! Your clothes are all over the floor. Your contact lens stuff and cosmetics all over the bathroom!"

"You!" She threw up her chin and glared at him.

"Who did you expect, *chère,* Prince Charming?"

"Certainly not with you aboard!"

"So you're feeling better?"

She nodded weakly, grumpily. "Not that much better." She dragged her fingers through her mussed hair. She still felt weak, and the patch made her sleepy.

"You'd better get up. You're in my bed, hogging my pillows, the covers. If you stay there much longer, I might decide to join you."

He made a move toward her.

"I—I'm getting up." That was wrong. She was fairly springing out of the bed. When his eyes raked her body, she snatched the sheet from him and pulled it around her.

He laughed in a superior, male way at that show of modesty. "Good. As I said, it's time you started earning your keep. I imagine you would prefer to earn it in the galley... rather than in the bedroom."

"As if those are the only places a woman belongs!"

"On this boat they are."

His expression altered subtly. His gaze ran from the curve of her slender neck down to the swell of her breasts. Her skin felt hot—almost as if he'd actually touched her. How did he do that with just his eyes?

"You belong in the dark ages."

"Most women who have sailed with me have not objected."

How dare he mention other women! It infuriated her that she cared. She glared at him fiercely. He grinned smugly at her obvious jealousy.

She remembered the way he'd clung to his edge of bed for hours and ended up on the floor. Then it came to her—he was deliberately baiting her. Why...he was bluffing. He was as afraid of seducing her as she was of being seduced. She turned this pleasant thought over in her mind. Her abductor was afraid of her, and he was covering it up with a bluster of sexist insults, hoping to rile her. What would happen if just this once she turned the tables on him?

She ran a hand through the fiery tangles of her hair, fluffed them, and let the radiant tendrils fall against her ivory cheeks. Remembering that he had always liked her shape, she tossed the sheet she'd been cowering behind to the bed so that the slim curves of her body were revealed.

"What are you doing?" he demanded in a hoarse low tone.

"I'm not much of a cook. Maybe...like those other women...I prefer the bedroom. You said I was...good. You were good, too."

At his dark frown, she smiled sweetly, lowered her fiery head and seductively peered at him through the thick, lush curls of her lashes. Then she got on the bed and crawled across it toward him, slowly like some hot

wanton tigress on the prowl. She'd seen a movie star do
it in an R-rated movie.

"Dear God. What are you doing?"

When she saw that his hand was trembling, she felt a
fierce gleeful satisfaction. "You can have me," she
whispered, moving her face very close to his. "If you
want me." She made her voice huskily musical.

She remembered how he liked her voice. She remembered all the things that he liked.... He was so close, she
could feel his warm breath brush her sensitive skin.

She saw his fear of her. Then she saw something
stronger than fear. His black eyes ate her, devouring her
with a dangerous consuming passion.

Just for a second, her heart fluttered against the inside of her chest like a bird's frightened wings against
its cage. She paled, terrified she'd gone too far.

With superhuman effort he tore his eyes away. "I'd
rather have breakfast," he growled. Then he threw open
the door and stormed out.

She collapsed onto the bed, weak with relief.

Eva opened the door to the main cabin and, clinging
to the wall, tried to ooze out of it, but this attempt at a
seductive slither was wasted because Nicholas didn't see
it. She saw him, though. The bathroom door was ajar,
and he was inside, stripped to the waist, with nothing on
but a pair of sexy, snugly fitting, faded jeans. His lower
face was a lather of white foam, and he was cutting
away dark morning stubble with quick, deft strokes of
his razor. His ink-dark hair was damp and slicked
back—he must have run a wet comb through it.

The motion of the boat was not nearly so terrible as
it had been the night before, but it was constant. He had

to brace himself to stand. It obviously took great skill to shave under such conditions.

He had always been good with his hands. That single thought induced vivid, sensual memories that made her shiver.

He didn't know she was there. Mesmerized, she watched him for a second. He was such a virile specimen of manhood with his trim hips and broad shoulders that he would be dangerous for any woman to be around for very long. But he was especially dangerous to her.

Her gaze was drawn to the tangle of scars that ran the length of his back. What kind of inhuman monster had beaten him so mercilessly? Her eyes misted at the thought of the pain he must have endured. She doubted if he had ever cried out, if he had ever let on how he suffered. No, she was sure he had stood it with the same grim fortitude he had stood all the other hard things in his life—his mother's death, his father's rejection, Africa, even... Yes, even her foolish, long-ago determination to try to remake him into a weak shadow of the vital man he was. Why hadn't she seen she had loved him as he was?

He had a fierce primitive strength. Maybe that was what drew her to him. She didn't know. But there was a bond. A bond so strong that eight years hadn't destroyed it. Nor had the most terrible scandal, nor her conservative family's fierce disapproval, nor the foolish mistakes they had both made in their relationship.

The network of scars was terrible, but to her they only made him more ruggedly beautiful. She longed to reach out and touch them, to offer him comfort for the pain she knew he had suffered. But he didn't want comfort from her. So she had to content herself with watching the play of his muscles as he moved the razor back and forth and then washed his face with water. Just watching him sent tremors of excitement through her.

When Nicholas, caught unawares, turned and found her there, he shifted uncomfortably. Flushing darkly, he reached for his shirt.

"It damned sure took you long enough," he muttered. "Did you make the bed?"

Not the most encouraging of overtures.

She smiled at him anyway because he had always been susceptible to her smile. "No, I was such a mess myself, I forgot."

His eyes swept over her with a hot, dark look that told her she was a mess no more.

"You and everything you have anything to do with," he grumbled.

His insult didn't bother her. He was neat to a fault, and she knew she looked nice with her hair tied back by a saucy lavender ribbon. She was wearing her silky lavender bathing suit that molded her body like a second skin. Her angelic face was scrubbed clean of salt grit, her lips moistened with lipstick that matched her suit.

Lavender had been his favorite color on her.

"Couldn't you have picked something else to wear?"

"What's wrong with what I'm wearing?"

"As if you don't know. It's tight and sexy, and you're alone on this boat with two men."

"Whose fault is that?"

"I'm warning you, *chère*, don't play with me. You may find out you're playing a game that you'll lose."

"Yes, I know." She just smiled. But her stomach danced with excitement. It was such sweet revenge to

taunt him for a change. Indeed, it was the only pleasure available under these trying circumstances.

"I'm starved," he said curtly.

"For breakfast?" she asked charmingly in her most
musical tone. "Or for. . ." She batted her lashes.

"For breakfast, damn it."

But neither of them was entirely sure.

"Well, I can't cook. I thought we'd decided I'm a
bedroom girl."

He ignored her last sentence and responded to her
first.

"It figures that you can't cook."

"What do you mean by that?"

"I mean you're messy as hell, disorganized, too.
Spoiled rotten by too many servants and a doting family. But it's time you changed. You're an adult. It's time
you stood on your own two feet."

"I have Connoisseurs."

"No, your father's money bought that, and his
money's bailed you out again and again. Every time
you've gotten in trouble with a man or your shop, the
Martins come to the rescue. You're so sweetly rotten, I
wonder if you can do anything for yourself. You're
marrying Otto so he'll take care of you and finance
Connoisseurs."

Stung to the core, she shouted back. "I wasn't going
to marry him!"

"Then why were you wearing his ring? I heard him
announce the engagement with my own ears."

"He wasn't supposed to do that."

"Sure." Nicholas's face was white and still, his eyes
red-rimmed from fatigue. "If you weren't going to
marry him, then you damn sure were leading him and
the rest of the world on."

"You once said I didn't believe in you. Well, you never believed in me, either! I'm telling you the truth."

For a moment something flared in his eyes, then vanished, and she saw that he wanted to believe her, but couldn't. "It doesn't matter," he said grimly.

But it did to her, more than anything. Suddenly tears welled in her eyes, silly ridiculous tears. She wiped her eyes, not wanting to cry. Not now!

"Look," he said, more on her side than he would ever readily admit. "I'm sorry. Your life is really none of my business. Believe me, I would have left you to it if I'd had a choice. I don't like this any better than you do. When it's safe, you and I will be done with each other for good. Can we just drop it? Zak and I are hungry. I wouldn't ask you to cook if we didn't really need your help."

Put like that, she was slightly mollified. But only slightly. Still, if she didn't cook for them, she would be acting spoiled and pampered.

He leaned down in front of her and lighted the stove for her.

"What do you want me to cook?"

He pulled out a box of dried eggs and put it on the counter. Beside the stove he set a loaf of bread, a pound of unopened coffee and a jar of marmalade.

"That ought to be easy enough for starters," he said dryly.

Easy? She stared at the two bare burners in desperation. How was she going to make toast—in a sauce pot?

Through the centuries other galley slaves had managed, most of them men, and everyone knew they weren't nearly so instinctually endowed with culinary talents as women. All she said was "Don't stay and watch me."

"I couldn't bear to." But he said it with just the flicker of a grin.

When she was done, she smiled proudly at the sight of her burned eggs until she saw that the galley looked like a dozen guerrilla soldiers had made war with eggs and marmalade. Spilled coffee was everywhere. Despite the gimbals, the eggs had slopped onto everything.

But if Nicholas minded the mess in the galley or the fact that the eggs were burned, he didn't say so. Below deck, at the table, he and Zak both ate the hot food with a gusto that pleased some secret female part of her nature that all feminists would deny even existed. The men seemed to savor every bite, while the electronic autopilot sailed the boat. The radar was turned on, and the men assured her that an alarm would go off if there was the slightest danger that they were on a collision course with a ship.

During the meal, Zak talked on the radio several times, and as always she watched and listened to him intently, carefully memorizing what he said about their latest position.

"Breakfast turned out rather well," Nicholas said when he was done.

She beamed.

"But then—I picked the menu."

As always he was impossibly conceited.

Victor, who looked like a drunken caricature of himself as he walked toward them at a decided slant, started to yowl at the sight of plates and food.

"Does he like sardines?" Nicholas asked her.

Sardines . . . She had managed to eat little breakfast, but at the mere mention of the word, her throat went dry and her stomach flipped queasily.

"I think I need . . . another patch for seasickness."

"Here." Nicholas pulled one from his pocket. "I'll open the can for the beast, to shut him up—even though it seems a terrible waste of good sardines."

She was too weak to defend Victor. Besides she wasn't altogether sure it was really necessary. Nicholas was going to feed him, wasn't he? So, instead, she went to the forepeak cabin and lay down so that she wouldn't have to smell the sardines.

Later Nicholas opened the hatches and aired out the boat for her. When she was feeling better he showed her how to work the saltwater pump so she could wash the dishes with seawater and thereby conserve their fresh water.

As he stood beside her in the galley, showing her how everything worked and where to stow things, she began to have the strangest feelings, dangerous feelings—like she belonged with him on this horrible boat, racing along in a stormy sea, with everything that mattered to her only yesterday not mattering to her at all today.

She hated the way he had taken control of her life, the way he had abducted her and carried her off on his boat. He was no better than a pirate, and yet for so many years she had longed for him. Every time she felt the dark force of his piercing gaze, or the accidental brushing of their bodies when the boat threw them together in the galley, she felt a quiver of spiraling excitement deep in the pit of her stomach that had nothing to do with seasickness.

Damn the man anyway! Intellectually she knew he was bad. But just standing beside him at the sink made her body react with a mind of its own. She felt tingly and soft and very feminine because he was so big and masculine. Beside hers, his hands were huge and darkly tanned. It was pleasant just to watch him dry a dish and put it neatly away. It was pleasant to breathe in the musky scent of his after-shave.

He was the bad guy.

What right did he have to be so virile and so awfully attractive?

But he said he'd come back to save her.

Paolo had beaten him.

Nicholas had risked his yacht, his own life, to take her away. He'd even gone back for her cat. More than anything she wanted to believe in him. It was difficult to imagine him sailing out into a storm just to recklessly amuse himself. But she'd never been any good at judging men, so she knew not to trust her instinct.

As he stood beside her, drying dishes, he was silent, seemingly unaware of her conflicting thoughts and emotions. When they were done with the dishes, he went up on deck to join Zak, closing the hatch because of the large swells.

Alone in the main cabin, she was still puzzling in confusion about Nicholas when the radio made a garbled sound.

The radio!

She was alone with it! This might be her only chance.

She scrambled across the bunks and table and grabbed the mike, hesitating only a fearful, breathless second. Then she flicked buttons and switches the way Zak had. Carefully she whispered into the microphone and made her distress call, giving the last position and heading she'd heard Zak give.

She waited as expectantly as an apprehensive child with a new toy.

Nothing. Frantic, she repeated the same call, terrified that Nicholas would open the hatch and discover her.

Metal slid against metal, and the hatch was flung open. A great whoosh of damp air sent charts flying everywhere. In the confusion, she hid the mike behind her back and glanced up innocently.

Zak's dark face was framed in the square of steel-gray light. She was so startled she nearly dropped the mike. Guilt over what she'd just done made her turn as white as paper.

"Oh, hi..." Her greeting was a croaky gasp.

Zak's dark gaze flicked to the radio and then back to her chalky face. "You don't look too good. You seasick again?"

She lied with a savage nod of her head.

"Why don't you lie down? I'll finish up in the galley."

Then he would come down. "N-no. I'm fine."

She wasn't though. She felt like a traitor—to Nicholas.

Nicholas's expression froze when he saw her step out of the cabin. The night was dark and moonless, but golden light from the open hatch backlighted Eva's hair and turned it to blowing flame. His fingers gripped the cold chrome wheel more tightly. She was beautiful, too beautiful.

All night, hour after hour, he had been clinging to the wheel, his deliberate intention to stay at the helm and avoid her by not going below.

She snapped the hatch shut, and they were alone together in the vast emptiness of the black night. Mist swirled around them.

"You must be dead," she said softly. "I brought you coffee. I made it the way you like it."

"Thank you." His tone was grim, but his fingers closed around the cup when she offered it to him. He felt the fleeting brush of her hand against his. Dear God, just her touch . . . just her being near . . .

Closing his eyes, he sipped the delicious hot liquid, but the warmth that spread through him was not from the coffee. It came from her presence. He wasn't used to anyone caring about his comfort. She paid too much attention to him. She noticed everything and did everything to try to please him. He was fastidious on board; she was messy by nature. But she had neatened the cabins, cooked and cleaned up after lunch and dinner. And everything she did made him more aware of her.

Not only was she turning into a most satisfactory crew member, but she was a pleasure to look at. Too much of a pleasure—in that tight lavender swimsuit that came so high on her thigh she seemed to be all curved golden leg. After the way she'd so wantonly teased him this morning—he knew now—just to bedevil him, he didn't trust himself to do the simplest thing with her without becoming aroused. Even teaching her to wash dishes had been a torment with her enticing body squeezed in the galley beside his, with the boat's movements causing too much accidental contact with each other. He had known then there was no way that he could spend another night in the same bed with her, without touching her—not unless he utterly exhausted himself first, which was what he had been doing for the past eight hours.

He'd liked having her on board, too much, which was dangerous. A single day had taught him what he'd been living without. He remembered the long months in prison, the trek across the desert, the years without her. Never had his life seemed so empty and lonely as it did now.

He had to remember he had taken her with him by force. She would never want him, never accept him, never believe in him. Nor could he allow himself to trust her. At any moment she might find a way to betray them to Otto.

He remained silent, determined to hold her at bay.

Naturally she couldn't leave it at that.

She inched carefully closer to him again, holding the lifelines, and he watched her lavender silk blouse ripple against her breasts. Always lavender... because she knew he thought she was beautiful in it.

Just watching her made his pulse begin to pound.

"How long before you let me go?" she queried softly.

Nicholas's gaze narrowed. "That depends."

"Surely you must see how impossible this whole situation is."

Oh, he saw.

"I can't stay. I have a life—"

"Which is why you *will* stay, so you will have that life. I don't like it any better than you do."

"What kind of man grabs a woman at a cocktail party and runs off with her?"

The muscles in his throat tightened. "I thought Otto told you what kind of man I was."

"Maybe I want to hear your side."

Her voice was like velvet. It made him want to pour out his soul.

His own low mutter was grimly rejecting. "That's a change."

"I do."

He stared past her. "You wouldn't listen."

"I listened before."

"To everyone but me."

"Tell me why you assumed a new name. I want to know about the scars on your back. About Africa. About everything. Please..." She put her hand very gently over his.

She was not forcing him to do anything, she was asking, sweetly asking. Maybe he owed her his side. Slowly he moved his fingers so that two of them were warmly entwined with hers.

"All right..."

After a long time he began, and in telling her, he became caught up in his tale. His voice grew low and furious as he drew vivid pictures of Africa, of the desert, of the hot, choking dust, of death, of blood and the flies. Hatred made him paint the horror of no medicine, the betrayal and the stench of the dying with hideous detail. He told her about the real Nicholas Jones, about Paolo, about the dreadful march from the battlefield to the prison, about the privations of thirst and drought he and Zak had had to endure to escape. He told her about his own fierce vow to obtain revenge when he learned Otto had killed his men and fed the press all the lies that had ruined his name.

When Nicholas finished, she was weeping. At the sight of her crying for him, some of his anger melted. His breathing slowed and his fists unclenched.

"Oh, Nicholas," she moaned softly.

He put his arms around her. "It was a long time ago." But he made an inaudible and very blasphemous curse.

"No, it's now."

He held her hard against his body until finally her sobs subsided and she stood quietly against him. With a sympathetic, healing touch she eased her hands over his back, her fingers tracing his bones and the coiled ridges of flesh that ran the length of his spine.

She drew in a deep breath and stifled a sob. "It must have been terrible."

His arm about her waist contracted. He told her more, everything, while she clutched him silently, willingly sharing the grim horror of it all. He described his bed of rock and sand in the prison, and how he'd lain on it every night torturing himself with dreams of home, of Louisiana, of food too—of mouth-watering delicacies like fried chicken, steak and baked potatoes. He didn't tell her that most of all he'd dreamed of her. He told her how terrible he'd felt when he'd found out Otto had bought Sweet Seclusion, and she'd remodeled it.

"Because I didn't know...I didn't know. In my heart I was restoring your home. Everything I bought, every board I had painted—I did it all for you. When I was finished, I went to London."

For a long time afterward they were silent as *Rogue Wave* soared over the black waves and left a wake of glistening phosphorescence. Eva's hair flew against Nicholas's cheek, and he breathed in the scent of honeysuckle and salt air. He did not know if she believed him, but her mere presence soothed the bitterness of his despair. No night at sea had ever been more beautiful than this one with its misty darkness, with her in his arms.

It was crazy to draw such pleasure in holding her, in talking to her. Wrong in a dozen ways. But confiding in her had brought a strange peace to him. Caution told him he should send her below, that any emotional closeness with her was dangerous, but the compulsion to go on holding her was too strong.

Despite the warmth of his arms about her, he forced a new hardness to come into his voice. "I lost everything—maybe because I was too soft, too trusting. My men, my good name, my soul, even you. All that is left of me is a savage desire for revenge against Otto."

"So you took me."

The gentle accusation was like a blow.

The little fool! Had she heard nothing then? Did she have no concept of what murder was? He could have shaken her.

Deliberately he dropped his arms from her shoulders, but she didn't move away. She was so close he could feel the heat of her body. He gripped the wheel. "Not exactly. I started a war. You got in the line of fire. I had no choice but to take you."

A desperate tension filled him. "Believe me, having you on this boat is the last thing I wanted."

That stung her. She backed away. "If you don't take me home, you'll ruin my life all over again."

"There are always casualties of war," he replied with careful indifference.

"The hundred men who followed you—is that all they were?"

Everything in him went as still as death. His dark eyes glittered.

"Are you going to let Africa ruin everything you were?"

"Shut up," he snarled, indifferent no longer.

"I loved you. I thought you loved me. I made mistakes, and I've regretted them. But you've made them, too. You weren't a quitter then. It's as if you've given up on life, on what's beautiful about it. Is there nothing left...of Raoul? Of that wonderful man I loved even though I never knew quite how to handle him?"

Why did she have to be so damnably beautiful? Why did her delectable mouth have to look so inviting? Why did she ask questions that tormented his very soul?

"Nothing."

"I think you lie." She came very close again, standing only inches from him. "You remember me." Then she touched him. As no other woman could, with fingertips of flame that beguilingly traced sinew and corded muscle.

Yes, there was the memory of her and this feverish longing that refused to die even though he knew the world was a dark place and that such feelings were pointless.

She let her hand fall away, but he was mesmerized by the aftermath of its spell. His body raged to give up the helm, to know the velvet, encasing warmth of her, to hold her tightly. He'd gone through hell to get back to her, only to find she was lost to him forever, but he'd never forgotten the splendor of her love and passion.

When she spoke again, her voice was so soft he could barely hear her. "The women you've had, did you ever fall in love with any of them?"

He laughed harshly. He thought of Anya, whom he'd planned to use in his plot of revenge, but Eva had given him his chance. "Love. You taught me the dangers of that trap. Never again. Women are to be used for the pleasure of satisfying an appetite."

He saw the desperate hurt in her eyes before she turned away.

"Let me go," she pleaded softly. "I promise that if you do, I'll run away—somewhere Otto will never find me."

"I can't take that risk."

"You don't care about me."

She turned away to leave him.

A sane man would have let her go.

Instead he uttered a low angry oath, secured the wheel and jerked her to him. His fingers embedded themselves in the thick waves of her hair. "No, I don't care," he muttered fiercely in a gravelly undertone that was unfamiliar to them both. "I don't care... At least not in the way a woman like you wants a man to care. You're like a fever in my blood, a disease that's devouring me from the inside out."

As he talked his hands were moving on her skin, sliding beneath her fluttering blouse, handling her with a rough expertise that left her gasping. "I want to hate you or to forget you, but ever since I saw you in Otto's stateroom, I haven't thought of anything else but taking you."

"Please... just let me go. Let me off this boat and we'll both come to our senses."

"It's too late." His fingers found her breasts, closing over the soft mounds of flesh. "I've lost mine completely. You're like a dangerous drug, and my craving for it is too strong." His jaw was set in a ruthless line. "I can't let you go. He will kill you."

Nicholas forced her back against the cabin, steadying himself and her. Then his mouth crushed down upon hers, silencing her murmurs of protest. Her hands splayed helplessly against his broad chest, Eva was trapped between the solid muscled wall of his powerful body and the wall of the cabin.

"Raoul." There was an unspoken plea in the way she said his name, her last futile attempt to stop him.

His hands roamed her body, noting that her breasts and hips were fuller, her waist slimmer. She was not so untried or girlish as she had been. She was a woman, fully formed. He was a man fully roused. She had teased him and beguiled him. What did she expect him to do?

She squirmed to resist him. She wouldn't have done it if she'd known that every move sent a jolt of electricity down the hard columns of his thighs.

"Be still," he growled, "Or we'll never make it to the bed."

From the cabin came two loud, frantic squawks.

Damn it to hell! The radar's alarm!

Directly ahead he saw the horror of red and green and white running lights. They were dangerously close! A giant black freighter loomed out of the misting darkness.

Nicholas jerked free of Eva, raced to the wheel and spun it fast and hard to starboard.

"Tacking!" he screamed.

The jib was cleated and backing. He rushed forward and released it. The big sail crackled wildly across the foredeck. He wrapped the sheet around the winch and trimmed.

Then he saw her white face. Her gold-brown eyes glittered opaquely as the freighter bore down on them. *Rogue Wave* seemed dead in the water.

Eva screamed and flung herself toward him, ready to die in his arms.

The freighter's bow wave crashed toward them, a deadly surge of white froth.

Seven

Eva was safe from the ship.

But not from Nicholas.

Still quaking from the near miss, she lay in the dark listening to the waves slosh against the hull, knowing he would come to bed soon, and dreading it.

The aft hatch opened. She heard Nicholas inside issuing curt orders to Zak; then she heard Nicholas's heavy footsteps treading across the teak floor toward the forepeak cabin.

Nicholas hesitated at the threshold. Every nerve in her body went off like an alarm bell when his hand twisted the brass latch.

Her blood ran cold.

Or rather, hot.

She was suffocating in this airless room with a hot, tense excitement.

The door banged open, and he was inside, filling the tiny room with his presence, stumbling on his bad leg as he groped in the blackness for the light. A shiver of apprehension raced over her flesh. Tonight he did not creep inside and pretend to ignore her. She wished there was someplace she could run to or hide, but the yacht was like a prison, and the deep water that surrounded it was more confining than the highest walls.

He hit his hand against the tiny fan bolted to the wall and cursed loudly and most descriptively before he finally managed to yank the lamp switch. The teak cell was instantly bathed with golden light.

She pretended to be asleep, but through her lashes she could watch him. His dark hair was windblown; his face was gray with exhaustion. Despite her fury and her despair, she ached because of the hard determined loneliness she sensed in him.

"That was close," he muttered grimly, ignoring her pretense of being asleep and loudly unsnapping his foul-weather jacket. "We missed her by no more than two hundred yards. Too close."

Yes. Silently she agreed with him.

He was speaking of the ship. She was thinking of his kiss, of the collision course their relationship was on.

"But close doesn't count."

It did to her. Especially now that they were alone together and would share the same bed for the rest of the night; especially now that she knew how completely changed he was from the man she had once loved. All day she had tried to please him. She had cooked. She had cleaned. She had listened to him when he'd talked about Africa and tried to understand all that he had been through. But this man was not the man she had loved.

Nicholas Jones was a stranger, determined to shut her out. It was as if he preferred to live in his world of darkness and deny that there was any other way to live. She was not a human being to him. All she could ever be was a pawn in the game he was playing with Otto or a temporary object of lust. She was on board Nicholas's boat. He was a man, she a woman who could serve a purpose for him any other woman could serve.

Through her lashes she kept a wary eye on his every move. She watched him hang his foul-weather jacket neatly on a hanger, strip off his boat shoes one by one, then his socks. Tidily he laid his socks and shoes on the shelf to dry.

Was this all that remained of him—a man who went through the mechanical motions of being a man? A man who was fastidious about his person, his boat—his *things*. A man who made vast sums of money in a complex, high-stake, international business while he played a deadly game of revenge. He could have written the owner's manual on any technical piece of equipment aboard *Rogue Wave*. He could sail her as though she were a part of himself. But when it came to being a real person...

He peeled off his shirt and jeans, and she gasped. Her pulse began to throb unevenly at the primitive, earthy, masculine vision. The less he wore, the more stunning he looked. When he sank down on the bed, she began to tremble with an emotion she understood all too well. Just his nearness cast a powerful pagan spell.

She stiffened, wary. She could not let his physical appeal blind her to the kind of man he had become. He had said that he used women solely for the pleasure of satisfying an appetite, and she now believed him.

If she had had any illusions, his violent kiss had dispelled them. Raoul was lost to her. The man Raoul had become, Nicholas, was so hardened he could never love again. He could only take and use, and destroy her all over again.

She remembered his harsh words and laughter with a sharp pang of guilt. "Love. You taught me the dangers of that trap."

Had she? Was she the cause of all that had gone wrong?

Years ago, Raoul had loved her desperately, and she had used her power to try to change him. He'd been a reckless entrepreneur, a brilliant maverick. But she hadn't appreciated his rare brand of talent, nor his courage to stand apart from the mainstream and excel. She had been so young, so incredibly foolish, too young to understand that loving someone did not give her the right to remake him. But hadn't she constantly tried to remake herself into the kind of person her family wanted her to be? Why would such an insecure person apply any different tactics to her love? She had believed she was helping him.

When her family had objected to his career, Eva had foolishly asked him to consider a more gentlemanly occupation, one like banking or medicine or law. He had laughed in her face at first and said a scoundrel would be a scoundrel whatever his trade and that an honorable man would behave honorably in any career, that he was good at his job, and happy in it.

If only she could have left it at that. Eva buried her head in her pillow but she couldn't escape the haunting memories.

After she'd succeeded in hounding Raoul into applying to law school just to please her, Eva's sister Noelle had suddenly ruined everything by becoming pregnant. At the time, it had seemed expedient that Noelle marry Garret Cagan and quickly. Since the Martins had disapproved of Garret as well as Raoul, the two sisters had decided that Eva should postpone her engagement to Raoul in order to spare their frail grandmother two misalliances at once. Eva had been so sure Raoul would be understanding. How could she have misunderstood him so completely?

She had hurt him and enraged him. Raoul had been so furious he'd hotheadedly leapt at the chance to rush off to Africa to check on Otto's oil fields. Eva remembered too well his last bitter taunt. "You know, *chère,* what really scares me is how close you came to remaking me into some whey-faced, namby-pamby hypocrite. I'd rather take a bullet in Rana."

Everything else had gone wrong after that. Noelle's baby had died. *Grand-mère* had had a stroke. Noelle hadn't married Garret, at least not then. Instead she'd run away to Australia. The Martins had covered up the scandal. Then war had broken out in Rana. A single letter had come from Raoul—he'd promised to be home for her birthday—to talk things out. Instead news of his death and treachery had come.

Her family had tried to be sympathetic. Otto had come around frequently to console her. When she'd remained depressed, they'd encouraged her to move to London and put the whole unfortunate affair behind her.

For so many years Eva had tried to forget Raoul. Now she couldn't help but realize that if she had believed in him and accepted him, he might never have gone to Africa. In a way, everything that had gone wrong in his life was her fault. If he was hard and bitter—if he was a killer, even—who had sent him to that fate?

Nicholas Jones snapped the chain on the lamp.

At the metallic sound, fresh pain splintered through her nerves.

The bed was shrouded in darkness.

The silent man and woman were as mute as two strangers, unable to sleep, unable to speak.

Eva's nerves tensed at his every sound, too conscious of the strength and animal fascination of him. His breathing seemed unusually harsh, and he twisted and thrashed like a great imprisoned beast, yanking the covers away from her, time and again. Rolling restlessly back again to his original position, he would throw them off.

She remembered his strong body crushing her against the cabin wall, her hair blowing against his face in the darkness, his hot lips against hers, devouring her mouth. He had admitted his fierce physical need of her. He was a hard, inhuman man. She kept dreading the time when he would reach out and take her—against her will.

An hour passed, and when his great body remained tensely coiled, as far from her as possible, gradually her fear of him lessened, and she began to weep silently for all that they had lost.

He lay beside her, still as stone, alert as a panther.

A strangled sob broke this silence. *Mon dieu.* To cry now... Why did the tears always come at the worst possible moment? She buried her hot wet face in a wadded pillow so it wouldn't happen again.

"Eva..." His tortured, raspy voice flowed across the darkness, infinitely soft.

She didn't dare answer him for fear he would hear the sound of more tears in her voice, but she cried so hard her whole body was wracked with sobs.

Tentatively he edged nearer. Too upset to reply, she could only sense the nearness of his body, the warmth and power of him.

"Chère..."

He touched her hair, stroked the long silky waves.

"I—I didn't want to bother you." Her voice was a small choked sound. She tried to keep her face buried so he couldn't feel her cheeks, but he loosened her fingers, prying the pillow free and tossing it to his side of the bed.

"Pillow pig," he whispered gently. "You had both of them, you know. No wonder I couldn't sleep."

His hand curved along her slender throat, turning her face slowly toward him. His lips brushed her cheeks, kissing away the salty tears, one by one. She held her breath, not needing air, if only his mouth would continue its sensual exploration of delicate skin and bone.

She licked her lips, wanting him to kiss her there, but although his mouth hovered close, he didn't. Instead he pulled her into his arms, sliding her smaller body so that it fit beneath his, and cradled her until she quieted.

"I'm sorry for what I did, for what I said," he murmured in a low husky tone.

"Don't..." She put two fingers against his lips.

Involuntarily her two fingers trailed downward, tracing the hard firm curve of his chin, the line of his jaw. When a fingertip touched his earlobe, she heard his deep, indrawn breath.

She withdrew her hand.

A long hushed silence fell. They just lay there, her body nestled beneath his, the rhythmic rolling of the boat seductively moving them together. The hard feel of his naked flesh against her smaller shape rocked her senses. She felt the heat of his breath against her throat, the musky scent of him enveloping her.

Not that he was any more immune to her than she to him. She felt his pulse begin to pound. His arms fell away, and she knew that he clenched his hands into fists to resist the temptation of deepening their embrace.

She had always been bold, but only with him. So she touched him as only she knew how. With wanton fingertips of flame.

On a groan he rolled over, pulling her on top of him so that her hair spilled over his perspiring face and shoulders, long satiny strands of it sticking to his skin.

"Are you sure?" His raspy voice was unsteady.

She felt him shaking with desire while she pretended to consider.

The emotion-charged seconds ticked by like hours while she held him in thrall. His dilated pupils filled his eyes and made them midnight black.

Then she leaned down and flicked his earlobe with her tongue, her fingers curled into the wavy thickness of his hair.

"I think so," she sighed at last.

"You think so, huh?" But he laughed throatily, and the deep vibrant rumble was as beautiful as music.

Because it was Raoul's laughter.

When he drew her face down gently to his, it was with Raoul's lips that he kissed her. The hands that undressed her and played over her body with reverent expertise were Raoul's hands as well.

She released a quivering pent-up sigh of complete surrender.

A wild hunger swept them both.

Sex had always been good between them, but this was different. Fiercer, hotter. When he'd lain in prison with his leg so infected he thought he'd surely lose it, he'd held on to his sanity only by dreaming of her in his arms. For her he was the passionate lover she had lost and found again.

There was a ferocity in them both that neither had ever known before. His tongue licked its way down her slim body, tickling her nipples, delving into her navel, until she lay beneath him, all hot and quivering, her eyes blazing, her shaky voice begging him to take her.

He moved on top of her, only to draw back stunned at her whimper when he found difficulty in entering her. She held him close, her fingertips pressed into his spine, and whispered fiercely, "it's only because...there has never been anyone but you. Only you."

She'd been a virgin the first time. But this was better, infinitely better. He touched her cheek tenderly and murmured something in French that was low and inaudible. Then he was inside her and there was pleasure, immense shattering bursts of pleasure that saturated their minds and hearts. They were twisting and writhing, and everything that had gone wrong between them was forgotten in that one final melting explosion of ecstasy.

He gathered her to him closely, and she fell asleep cradled in his arms with the joyous knowledge that at last everything was going to be all right.

Early the next morning, Nicholas stood at the helm, coldly oblivious to the perfection of the sparkling morning. All trace of the storm had vanished from the skies and seas. Directly ahead he saw his island floating like a dazzling white jewel in a turquoise sea. The salty air blowing off the fringe of cliffs brought the scents of basil, bougainvillea, pine, and all the unidentified herbs Marcos planted every spring. At any other time the scene would have seemed paradisiacal, but this morning the bleached dome with its plunging cliffs loomed before Nicholas like the worst hell on earth. How many days—how many nights—would he be trapped there with Eva?

Nicholas was furious with himself. By sleeping with her he had complicated the hell out of an already complicated situation. He had planned to spend a week with her at most and be done with her forever.

She was still asleep. Thank God for that. He lighted a cigarette and carefully shook out the match. If only there was some way he could do as she'd asked and let her go in some safe harbor—but she didn't really understand the full extent of the danger. If she returned to London, one of Otto's men would be there to kill her. Nicholas had no choice but to stay with her and wait it out until he was sure she would be safe. Once Otto failed to make his interest payments later in the week, he would be receiving so much notoriety that he'd be afraid to make a false move.

Last night Eva had felt so good. Nicholas got aroused just thinking about it. He took a long pull on his cigarette, not wanting to torture himself by remembering. But it was no use. The memory of her arms and legs wrapped around him, of her muted cry of passion at the end, had driven him wild.

Grimly he pitched his cigarette into the water and turned the wheel hard alee so he could sail around the island once to make sure there were no other unwanted visitors moored offshore. When the main sail swung across, he tightened the sheet.

As he got closer to shore, he forced himself to concentrate on the island, noting how the rare sheltered folds of ground where Marcos cultivated the vines were unusually lush and green. But instead of the island, Nicholas kept remembering the erotic vision of Eva in his bed with her hair fanning across his pillows like a wreath of flame, with the sheet molding her shapely body.

His throat went dry.

The ruin of the Roman village at the foot of the cliffs came into view. He scarcely gave it a thought. Nor was he in any mood to admire his stunning house, which had been designed by one of the most famous architects in the world. The top floor of the mansion capped the island; the lower floors were carved into the side of the cliff.

Nicholas had chosen the island as the perfect hiding place because no one knew that he owned it. The house was equipped with sophisticated electronics—telexes, computers, fax machines, a network of telephone lines—everything he needed to conduct his business and stay abreast of what was happening.

The house was easily accessible to the water; paths led down from the terraces of the house to the beaches and natural swimming pools. More importantly there was a magnificent cave beneath his home that covered the deepest of these natural pools. There was a hidden elevator cut through solid rock cliff inside the cave. The cave's ceiling was high enough to moor and conceal *Rogue Wave* even with her tall masts. There was also a narrow cliff path within the cave that led to the house so that a man could go up and come down without being seen from the water or air.

Nicholas always came here alone. The island was a very romantic setting, the worst kind of environment to spend time with a woman a man wanted to avoid.

Not that Nicholas hadn't known this would be a problem. From the moment he'd seen Eva bathing in Otto's stateroom, the sight of her in that tub had stirred every repressed erotic male fantasy he had ever had of her.

Last night when he'd gone to bed it had taken a superhuman effort to leave her alone. Then she'd cried, the sound of her heartbroken tears luring him into her arms. Once there, he'd been lost.

Now he realized it was as clear as day that she'd known exactly what she was doing. She had known he had wanted her and yet all of yesterday she'd deliberately teased him.

She probably thought she had the upper hand now. But she was wrong.

Once, years ago, he had longed for Eva's love and a normal life with her, longed for it so cravenly that he had almost been willing to allow her to remold him in the image she had of the ideal man, until she'd shown him that no matter how he changed, he would never be acceptable. If he hadn't been good enough for her then, he damned sure wasn't now. He was too old to change, too old to risk his heart again—if he still had one.

The entrance of the cave was very close. Nicholas started the auxiliary engine and switched on the depth finder. When he put the engine in gear, the clutch slipped. Damn. He'd have to get Zak to check that.

Nicholas pointed the boat into the wind and hollered down below for Zak, who leapt up at once, racing to the foredeck to take down the jib while Nicholas lowered the main. Then they pulled out anchors and line and made them ready. Zak grabbed the boat hook to fend off from the walls of the cave as Nicholas slowed the yacht and headed it toward the tunnel of limestone walls.

The channel into the cave was narrow and cut through rock reef, its depth so uncertain in places that Zak had to call out constant readings from the depth finder.

"Twenty feet."

Rock walls on either side of the cave's entrance jutted dangerously close on both sides.

"Fifteen."

Nicholas cut the power.

"Seven!"

The *Rogue* drew five. Nicholas had to steer very carefully to keep her in the center of the channel so her keel wouldn't scrape bottom.

"Six!"

His breathing stopped. At just that moment, the worst of all possible moments, Eva emerged from the cabin to distract him.

"Five and a half!"

"Good morning," she whispered dreamily, looking lovely and sleep-mussed, her eyes softly aglow as she smiled at him, her red tangled hair glistening in the sunshine as the breeze blew it about her shoulders. She was wearing that bathing suit again that fit—what damned little of her body it covered!—like a silky lavender glove. Nicholas could see jutting nipples, everything—except where to steer. Standing amidship, her exquisite body completely blocked his vision of that. He felt a warm jolt of pleasure at the sight of her and then fury and panic.

"Five and a quarter," Zak yelled.

Terror gripped Nicholas.

"Damn it! I can't see through you! Get below," he yelled at her, cold anger in his voice, "before I wreck her."

The beautiful happiness in Eva's face died instantly. She went white, his harsh words like a blow. The bright tousled head disappeared below.

Zak shot him a peculiar look. Nicholas told himself there was no way he could know what had happened between himself and Eva. No way.

"Five and a half. Seven."

They were over the reef. They were safe—inside the shady concealing coolness of thick limestone walls, the ship's white hull seeming to hang suspended over the crystal-clear waters.

"Twenty-five."

Nicholas saw Eva hovering uncertainly halfway down the stairs, her beautiful face ashen, her lovely eyes blurred by tears. Deliberately Nicholas made his voice even rougher. "Well, don't just stand there. Come up and help Zak with the dinghy while I set the anchors."

Without a word, she came up, turned her back on him and helped Zak lower the dinghy at the stern and tie and secure the painter. Zak was unusually nice to her.

And that grated, too. Especially when Zak called her to the foredeck to help stow the jib. Not that Nicholas thought she could be of much real help. But Zak was so patient and instructive that soon she was hanking the halyard to the mast, bagging the sail, and coiling lines like an expert, with Zak complimenting everything she did so excessively he had Eva beaming and Nicholas scowling.

Zak went below and helped her prepare breakfast. At the easy camaraderie between them, Nicholas ground his teeth. If Zak was going to cook, he'd have to see to the clutch himself.

Nicholas's bad leg throbbed from the awkwardness of squeezing himself into a tiny corner of the aft cabin so he could get to the engine. In the galley Zak and Eva laughed and talked.

Nicholas tried not to watch them or listen, but every time Zak smiled at her, every time she laughed at something he said, the knot inside Nicholas's gut wound a little tighter.

By the time the three of them sat down to breakfast together, Nicholas was green with jealousy. He had wanted her to ignore him. Well, she was ignoring the hell out of him. And seemingly enjoying the hell out of herself while she did so. She passed Zak the marmalade, not noticing that he hadn't had any himself.

Nicholas sat silently eating the unburned eggs and noted that her cooking was better. She was a quick learner, and for some reason that made him even madder, her virtues annoying him even more than her faults. Throughout the meal, Nicholas endured the friendly chatter of his woman and his best friend, his grim tension building like a storm cloud.

As the morning wore on, things got worse.

Nicholas wanted to ignore her, but whatever she did, she had his undivided attention. She sang a French love song as she washed the dishes, and her beautiful voice was such a distraction he couldn't do a thing with the transmission. Finally he threw his wrench down in frustration, and it hit his toe. Not that she so much as looked at him when he cursed about it. She never missed a note. In utter frustration he gave up on the engine and called Zak over to help him.

"Hey, don't act so riled. It's just the fluid, man. Here's the leak," Zak purred, his tone superior.

She heard.

"Then if it's so easy to fix, you do it," Nicholas growled, furious at them both.

Wisely Eva disappeared into the forepeak cabin, but Nicholas could hear her bustling about and couldn't forget she was there.

"So what are you going to do about her?"

Nicholas flashed his friend a dark look.

"I asked you a question."

Nicholas grimaced. "Which was none of your business."

"Hey, I have to live with the two of you. She cries. You sulk."

"That's your problem."

"That's why I'm asking you to do something about it."

Nicholas threw his oil rag to the floor, strode up the stairs and went outside, but Eva, who had opened the forward hatch and climbed out, was already up on the foredeck stretched out on a towel reading a paperback novel.

She never even looked up. Well, he damn sure wouldn't go back below just because she was there. That would only prove to her he'd noticed her.

Nicholas lowered a bucket and began to wash the cockpit with salt water and a brush. He was scrubbing so furiously he didn't hear her soft approach.

"Maybe it would help if I went ashore."

His black head jerked up. "What?"

The sunlight came from behind her, so he couldn't see how much her boldness was costing her—the quick flame of color in her cheeks, the overbright flare of hope in her eyes. All he saw was the dark outline of her body, the perfect female shape of her. All he felt was the unforgivable urge to drag her into his arms and make love to her violently. But that was a weakness he was determined not to give in to again.

"You heard me." Her voice was whispery, nervous. "My presence is obviously driving you crazy."

"The hell it is." A savage pulse had begun in his throat. "I don't give a damn about you one way or the other."

The sun blinded him. He couldn't see her whiten. "Well, then," she said with a calmness that infuriated him, "since it isn't, maybe we can start the morning over and try to have a normal conversation."

"I thought you were reading a book."

"I can't seem to get into it." Her voice was slow, husky, and somehow more unnerving than ever.

"Maybe you haven't tried hard enough."

"Maybe." She tossed it down and sank on her knees beside him, mindless of the book's pages fluttering in the wind. "Is this your private island? Or are we trespassing?"

Never had she shown him more naked golden skin... except last night. Damn it! He wasn't going to think about that. But her beautiful body was a soft coil of thighs, breasts arms, and he couldn't ignore her. What was she trying to do to him?

"Yes. It's mine."

"It's wonderful. Do you come here often?"

"Only in the summers."

"With friends?"

"Alone."

"Always alone?" she persisted.

"Damn it. I said it once, didn't I? I like being alone."
His last sentence was a careful insult.

"Oh, you do?"

Her voice was naive, innocent. It compelled him to
look at her. When he did, he felt the golden-brown
dazzle of her eyes seeking his. His blood began to beat
again, violently. "Look..."

"You could be alone if I went ashore," she said
composedly, looking at him through her lashes.

"No!"

"Why do you care, if you want to be alone so
much?"

"I don't, damn it!" What was he saying? "You're to
stay because I said so." Even to himself, his sharp answer sounded unreasonable, like that of a child.

She wouldn't drop it. "I thought I saw a house on top
of the island."

"The house is mine, too," he snarled.

"Can't we stay there?"

"No! A family lives there. Caretakers. A man, a
woman, and a child. Stay away from them."

"I've been on this boat for two nights and two days.
I want to go ashore. I want to stand up straight without
having to hold on to something. I want to walk on solid
ground."

It was a reasonable request, but he wasn't feeling the
least bit reasonable toward her.

"Look. This isn't some pleasure cruise. Otto will be
scouring the Mediterranean looking for us. If he sees
you, or any of us, everyone on the island could die—
including those people at the house. I want you near
me, where I can watch you."

"I thought I saw a path through the cave."

"It's too steep and slippery. If you don't know it well, you could fall. One of us would have to go with you." He didn't mention that the cave had a hidden elevator that only he had a key to.

"Then I'll ask Zak."

"You leave Zak alone!"

"Why are you doing this?"

"Because of the danger."

"No. I—I don't mean that. I mean why are you being so deliberately hateful? You've been awful, deliberately awful, all morning. Is all this... because of what happened last night?"

He couldn't see her tear-laden eyes, but he heard the sadness in her voice. And it stopped him dead. Then he told himself that she was doing it again, what she'd done last night, acting vulnerable, bringing out some insane masculine urge in him to protect her.

He wanted to take her in his arms again, to kiss away the tears, to ease the terrible pain he was inflicting, to tell her how much he wanted her. But when he spoke his voice was low and harsh. "I told you my feelings on the subject. Don't make last night something it wasn't."

"Then you just used me—to satisfy an appetite?"

He knew her softness could destroy him. He heard the break in her voice, but he made no denial.

"Oh, how could you?" He heard her sudden intake of breath. "And I thought..." Her voice trailed away, bleak, pain-filled.

"Why are you surprised, when you've always considered me a scoundrel?"

"No, I never did. And I don't think I ever really believed Otto. Last night, when you were kind to me, I almost believed that I'd been right about you all along, that I do have the instincts to judge good from evil in men. That there is some remnant of a decent human being left inside you. Oh, how wrong I was.''

The heartbreak and anguish in her voice cut through him like a knife.

"You want to be alone!" she cried. "Well, fine—be alone!"

He heard her misery through the mists of his own pain. He reached toward her, but he was too late. She leapt up, and before he could stop her, she climbed over the lifelines and sprang, her slim form arched in a perfect swan dive into the water.

"Eva!"

There was a splash and she disappeared into the deep blue depths. Then her bright head broke the surface, and she swam with swift deliberate strokes away from *Rogue Wave* toward the island—in deliberate defiance of him. She could have gotten out at a nearby rocky ledge in the cave, but she was too upset to notice. She was swimming through the channel for the beach outside the cave, the only other place a swimmer could emerge safely. It was a long swim, much of it through deep water. There were currents around the island and dangerous undertows. He remembered her terror of deep water, how close she had once come to drowning. She would never have jumped in if she hadn't felt desperate to escape him.

If anything happened to her...

He pulled off his shoes and tossed them into the boat. Then he dived in after her. He swam through the channel into open water, but she was nowhere in sight. When he reached the beach there was still no sign of her. He fought against the first flicker of panic. Where was she? She had to be somewhere near.

He yelled for her. Not a sound from her. Only the echo of his own voice. Nothing but empty beach, a great wall of bleached rock towering above him on one side and an endless expanse of blue sea stretching away from him on the other.

"Eva!" he called her name, and when she didn't answer, his mindless fear mushroomed. He hadn't seen her emerge from the water. Dear God. He squinted hard, staring out at the turquoise water sparkling beneath a brilliant sun. Finally he sank to his knees in despair. Had she already drowned? He would never forgive himself.

"I'm up here," she called down to him after a long time.

She was standing above him on a narrow ledge next to another opening to the cave.

She had been deliberately hiding from him!

He was furious all over again. "Come down, damn you!"

She glared down at him mutinously. When he started to come up, she slipped back inside the cave.

Wild with anger, he climbed recklessly up the rocks, cutting his feet, his hands, his legs, but not caring. When he reached the path, he followed her into the cave. Inside it was dark and cool. Blinded from the brilliance outside, he couldn't see a thing.

"I'm right here," she said softly.

He whirled.

To his surprise she was standing a few mere inches from him. She had been waiting for him just inside. He saw that the ledge behind her narrowed dangerously. She was trapped.

He caught her to him, gripping her arms so hard she cried out.

Flesh to flesh. Wetly hot woman skin turned his every male cell to fire.

"What the hell kind of game are you playing?" His voice cracked like a whip in the hushed silence of the cave.

Rage, relief that she was alive, passion—all these things were burning in him as he held her nearly naked body against his own.

She said nothing. A tremor went through her. It was as if she knew that she had pushed him as far as he could be pushed. She moistened her lower lip with the pink tip of her tongue. He watched the movement, fascinated.

He felt a swift hot stab of arousal. His eyes met hers only to lose himself in those whiskey-dark eyes that blazed with a need as fierce as his own.

With fingertips of flame she touched him.

And then he knew her game.

But it was already too late.

He pushed her against the wall, his body pressing into hers, and he kissed her until they were both breathless. Then he picked her up in his arms and carried her down the narrow ledge. She clung to him trustingly even when he stooped and took her into a low-ceilinged, hidden grotto.

There in that sheltered darkness, on a bed of cool wet sand they made love. Gently, completely. It didn't matter that he came from a brutal world that she couldn't understand. It didn't matter that she could never truly be his. Nothing mattered but the glorious explosion of ecstasy they found in each other's arms.

Eight

Enclosed within Nicholas's strong arms, Eva lay quietly beneath him, her beautiful face aglow with satisfaction.

He had fought the passion that bound him to her and lost, but he had no more rage for her, only wonderment that he had endured the long years without her. There could be no hope for a future. They had only today—at most perhaps the next day and the one after that.

A week—maybe.

The rest of his life to be lived in less than seven days.

Then she would be gone.

Nicholas put one hand on either side of her hot cheeks and with careful deliberation kissed her eyelids, the feathered black tips of her densely curled lashes; then her nose, her mouth.

She was sweet. Oh, so dangerously sweet.

She opened her languorous eyes, and for a few seconds they remained deliciously remote. Then she focused on him. "Nicholas," she whispered.

"Yes, *chère.*"

She touched his brow, smoothed back the black lock with the strands of silver from his brow. "I've made so many mistakes with you."

"So have I."

"If I'd only taken the trouble to really understand you." She paused. "Maybe—"

"Don't," he whispered. "No regrets..."

"I want to know everything about you," she persisted.

He smiled. "All the secrets of my scandalous life?"

She laughed. "Something like that."

"There are too many to tell."

"Just one then. When you were a teenager—why did your father really kick you out?"

His face tightened. She was digging deep. Too deep. He had to swallow hard to maintain control. "Why do you want to know about that?"

Eva softly kissed his cheek. "Because that's when everybody said you went bad. You never told me anything, and I was just a baby when it happened. All I've ever heard were the rumors. I can't believe they were true."

He tensed and pulled away from her, staring into the cave, his thoughts whirling away from the present, back down the dark corridor of time.

Dimly he heard her say, "You don't have to tell me, if you don't want to."

He didn't want to talk about it, but the gentle tenderness in her face and voice breached his defenses. She had a way of pulling the pain out of his soul and healing him with her kindness. His hand closed around a rock so hard it cut into his callused palm. "Which of the rumors did you hear?" His voice was rough with the effort it took to restrain all the old emotions and bitter resentments.

"That your father caught you in bed with your stepmother. You were only seventeen, she was twenty. Was it true?"

All the old hate and pain and fear boiled up in him. He remembered how lost he'd been when his father had thrown him out.

There was scorn in Nicholas's voice when he spoke. "In a way, I guess it was true. You've got the ages right. I had never lived around a woman. I resented it when my father married Louise. He changed after he married her. He had been bitter with me, spending his nights with the bottle on a downstairs couch. After Louise came, he was always laughing." Nicholas paused.

"They hadn't been married very long when it happened. One night she called me into her bedroom to look for her earring that she said had fallen between the wall and the bed. She had the sheets pulled over her, and I didn't know she was naked beneath them. My father came up the stairs, and she threw off the sheet and started screaming. He caught us there and assumed the worst. She told him that I tried to force her to make love to me. He believed her. He grabbed a belt and would have beaten the life out of me if I hadn't run away. Later, when he changed his will in favor of her baby son, I figured out why she did it. Sweet Seclusion came from my mother. I never saw him again."

"How awful."

"I learned early how it feels to be wrongly accused."

Tears of empathy sprang into Eva's eyes, and Nicholas clutched her to him. He told her of the wretched years that followed, how he'd drifted from one menial job to another, how he'd been picked up for vagrancy, how he'd been too wild, how he'd attempted and failed at college more times than he could count.

"Hell, it took me seven colleges, but I finally had the sense to stick it out and get a business degree. When I graduated at the top of my class, I decided that if I could do that, I could do anything. You know the rest."

Her arms were about him, holding him tightly. She caressed his shoulders, his neck. She combed her fingers through the curling darkness of his hair.

"There was never anyone for me," he said.

"Never until now," she whispered.

She held his hand so that her slim white palm fit into his larger, darker one. Even this gentle touching of their hands coming together sent a charge of electricity through them both.

Her palm was fragile and soft, his roughly callused. His fingers overlapped hers by inches. He could have closed his hand and easily crushed her delicate bones. Instead he slid his hand against hers and massaged the velvet softness. The warmth of her skin seeped into his.

The black-and-gold onyx ring gleamed on her finger, his long-ago gift of love to her when she'd been an innocent girl. He stared hard at the ring she'd pressed into his hand to keep him safe when he'd left her to go to Africa. "I will wear it forever," she had said, "when you bring it back to me."

Nicholas met Eva's gaze and saw love and an innocent trust shining there. He saw as well the pure beautiful strength in her heart and soul, her belief in the possibility of happiness, in the future, her faith in everything that was utterly lacking in him. She was that innocent girl again, but a woman, too. A woman who had loved and lost and yet still believed in the redeeming power of love.

He laced his fingers through hers more tightly and dragged her beneath him again.

"You feel good, Eva," he whispered. "So good, you almost make me whole." His mouth found her lips, and he kissed them briefly, with an ache that filled his entire being. "Don't make this into something it can never be. For us there will be no tomorrow."

Eva lay on the deck, her book closed beside her, her fingers restlessly tapping the cover. Beside her were a bottle of teak oil and a rag. She could hear Nicholas and Zak down below dismantling the transmission again, the leak having proved difficult to repair.

No tomorrow...

That meant he would say goodbye again.

How Nicholas's words had haunted Eva in the three days that had followed them. Three days of golden sun, three days of passionate lovemaking in their secret grotto and in his bed at night. Every time Nicholas touched her, every time he looked at her, she was aware that precious time was running out.

Nicholas was gentler with her now. Although he never spoke words of love or made any promises about what the future might hold, sometimes she caught him unawares, watching her with a sad tenderness in his eyes. The moment he saw she was watching, the poignant warmth would fade, and his old bleak mask would slip back into place.

Only when they made love was he different. Only when he was deep inside her would the mask slip away.

He would hold her tightly, as if he'd never let her go, his face rapt with pleasure. Then in the wild tumult of their passion he was completely hers.

Otto had not come. Nicholas was frustrated because there was very little about him in the news. The lazy drifting days that were filled with fishing and swimming and reading made it impossible for her to believe they were in any real danger, yet there was constant tension in Nicholas and Zak. She was never allowed out of their sight for long.

Every afternoon Nicholas went up to the house alone and spent long hours on the phone, at his computers. He left her with Zak, and she had grown so restless and bored on the boat in his absence that Zak had set her to polishing chrome and teak. Every time Nicholas left, she begged him to take her along. She wanted to be with him, to see his house, to meet the couple and the child that lived there. He always, gently but firmly, stepped into the dinghy without her. The one surprise was that he allowed Victor to go along. "I'd do anything to get him off the boat awhile," Nicholas had explained. Sometimes Victor would stay ashore only to make a nuisance of himself by returning to the cave's lower ledge around midnight and yowling. Nicholas would have to go get him then.

Eva decided the reason Nicholas didn't want her to go was because he must be afraid that she would try to use the sophisticated equipment at the house to contact the outside world. Which was the last thing she wanted to do—now. Guiltily she remembered those two unanswered calls for help she had secretly made.

From the beach every evening, Eva had watched the couple walking with their small son at the top of the cliff. The man and woman had golden hair and skin,

their son was slim and bronzed and black-headed. One
evening the young woman had looked down and seen
her. She had waved. Perhaps because the family was
forbidden to her, Eva was filled with curiosity about
them. She longed for female companionship, for
someone different to talk to. Eva imagined that such a
woman must be fascinating. Eva wanted to ask her what
it was like to live on an island, cut off from the world
with only her husband and child for company. Eva
longed to meet the little boy as well.

Every day Eva's curiosity and boredom and restless-
ness grew. Thoughts of the house and the family took
her mind off of Nicholas and their impossible relationship.

Eva's daydreaming was interrupted when high above
the boat where she lay on the topmost ledge in the cave
there was a sound. Then a rock splashed into the water
near *Rogue Wave*'s hull.

Eva's fingers froze on her book. She looked up and
saw the little boy and Victor together. The child, another rock in his hand, seemed to be staring down at her
with a curiosity equal to her own. Victor was beside
him. She called up to them. The child tossed the rock,
and it landed closer, near the dinghy like an invitation,
personally delivered.

She heard Nicholas curse down below. He was completely absorbed with his engine.

Was he her lord and master?

Not even considering such a silly question, she tip-
toed across the deck, loosened the knot in the painter,
and got into the dinghy as it slipped away. She glanced
up and saw that the boy and cat had vanished.

Rowing all the way to the beach, she dragged the
dinghy and its oars ashore and climbed the cliff. From

time to time she had to stop to catch her breath. The sun beamed down; the northwesterly, as Nicholas called the perpetual breeze, blew her hair. The world seemed an eternity of warm hazy sky and undulating turquoise. It was impossible to imagine that there could be any danger.

She was breathless when she reached the magnificent house. Its terraces commanded beautiful views of the sea and the rest of the island. There were fig trees and prickly pears, fleshily fanned. She saw the satellite dish, antennae of all sorts, all partially concealed behind a tumble of boulders.

The blond woman and her dark-haired boy were walking with Victor beneath a grove of olive trees.

Victor meowed loudly when he saw her.

The beautiful young woman, her face radiant with welcome, came over at once. She was flushed and smiling. "You are Nicholas's friend," she said in a softly accented voice.

"I'm Evangeline Martin."

"And I'm Teresa. This is Nickie . . ."

Nickie came forward. His white smile and black eyes were brilliant as he tentatively offered his hand. Evangeline knelt down and took it, but hardly had she touched his tiny fingers than they had flown from her grasp. He moved like lightning. He was a small child, no more than six, Evangeline imagined. He was incredibly lively.

"He must be a handful, with all the high cliffs and the cave," Eva said.

Teresa smiled, the kindly tolerant smile of a mother. "He loves the island. We come every summer with my brother. Marcos helps me watch him when he isn't fishing."

"Oh, I thought you lived with your husband."

A fleeting shadow passed over Teresa's beautiful face as she fingered the plain gold band on her left hand.

"I'm sorry if I said something wrong," Eva said.

Teresa's gentle, accepting smile was meant to reassure. "It's all right. Would you like some refreshment after your long walk up the cliff?"

"Water would be fine."

"I have homemade wine."

"That would be lovely."

Nickie was playing on the ground with Victor beneath the olive trees. They seemed to be old friends. While Teresa was inside, Eva watched them. Nickie got up. He had a white cane, which he tapped on the ground. Victor chased after him, leaping for the tapping cane and pawing it.

A white cane?

Was Teresa's beautiful boy blind?

Eva was suddenly horrified the child would trip. "Victor!"

"It's all right," Teresa murmured soothingly, setting her tray with a bowl of ripe figs, a decanter of wine and wineglasses on a low table. "It's one of their favorite games. They like to play in the cave, too. There's an opening just beyond the grove. If you know the way, you can climb all the way down to the water through the cave."

"Nicholas told me." Eva sipped her wine, which was sweet and dark, and she complimented it.

"My brother, Marcos, cultivates the grapes on the island," Teresa said.

Eva's attention was on the child and the cat. "Is Nickie blind? Wouldn't it be dangerous for him to go into the cave?"

"He's only partially blind. His doctor says in another year he can have an operation that will help him. He's spent all his summers here. Look, there go the two of them. Nickie knows the cliffs in there as well as he knows his own room. He loves it here." There was no trace of concern in Teresa's voice.

"Do you mind if I follow them—just to make sure Victor doesn't trip him?"

Teresa shook her head. "I'll come, too." Teresa talked amiably. She said, "I get so lonely to talk to another woman. I have been begging Nicholas to bring you up or pleading with him to let me come down."

"So have I."

"Nicholas can be very stubborn."

They laughed together.

Inside the cave, the cliffs were steep and treacherous, but Eva could see the path leading all the way to the sea. Nickie and Victor were snugly ensconced on a narrow ledge. She could see *Rogue Wave*'s anchor line. Inch by inch her gaze followed it from the water to the yacht. Nicholas was standing at the pulpit, and even in the shadowy cave, she saw that every line of his body seemed grim and hard with anger the moment he caught sight of her.

Quickly she looked away. Too quickly. Her foot slipped.

A rock tumbled down the cliff and hit the water. She watched its spiraling descent to the bottom of the pool. The cliff was so steep, the path so narrow, she was suddenly dizzy. The walls of the cave seemed to sway in lazy circles. Shakily she pressed her back against the cool limestone and clung. Beneath she saw the dark water. Then it blurred. Her balance was gone. Panic stabbed through her, and she screamed in terror, afraid she would fall.

She heard Nicholas shout far below.

The world seemed to fade into darkness, and she imagined herself sinking down, down into that pool. She was drowning—as before. Burning water was filling her throat. Her body was pulled through currents, drifting deeper and deeper. She was choking.

Then she heard Teresa, right beside her saying, "Hey, everything's okay." Teresa's hand gently took hers. "I think we'd better go back outside. I'll lead the way."

Eva opened her eyes. Teresa was so kind, so gentle, so understanding. Back at the house Eva told her that once she had nearly drowned, that for years she'd had a phobia about water, that she'd thought she was over it.

"Does Nicholas know?" Teresa asked.

"He was there when it happened."

"Then it seems odd that he would invite you on a cruise. He's usually so kind and thoughtful."

Eva could only stare at her. "Kind and thoughtful." Was that how Teresa saw him?

Teresa began to talk of her life on the island as well as her life away from it.

Innocently Eva asked, "Does Nickie go to school yet?"

"Oh, yes. Nicholas sends him to a special school every fall in London."

"Nicholas sends—" Eva's voice broke. She could only stare at Teresa in dumb shock. Nicholas was paying for her son's education. Why?

Nicholas. Nickie. The similarity of the two names hadn't clicked. Perhaps because to Eva Nicholas was Raoul. Teresa had said she lived with her brother, not her husband. The golden band on Teresa's hand glittered in the sunlight.

Teresa was married to someone.

And she was living in Nicholas's house.

Eva's imagination speculated wildly. Was that someone a man who would send his son to school but refused to live with his mother? A man so callous he
would bring another woman to the same island where
his wife lived? Was he making love to both of them?
Eva could not quite fathom that horror.

Why was she so surprised, Eva wondered?

But she was.

He had admitted to other women, to casual relation-
ships, but never to this. Nickie was small. He must be
around six years old.

It was all too easy to imagine what must have happened. Nicholas had returned from Africa and found
solace in this lovely woman's arms. There had been a
child, even marriage, although not a real one because
Nicholas had been too brutalized for anything else. He
had merely lived up to his responsibilities. Eva could
almost have forgiven him, if only he had told her. Almost.

Teresa was so beautiful and golden, so saintly. The
child could only have inherited his daredevil vitality and
his darkness from his father. No wonder Nicholas
hadn't wanted Eva up here. How could Teresa be so
kind and accepting of her? How many others had
Nicholas brought to the island?

Eva remembered the wanton ecstasy of Nicholas's
recent lovemaking all too clearly, his fevered mouth
against her skin, the torrid flow of excitement racing
through her veins as hot as a forest fire. He'd made her
wait and wait.

Their passion seemed a travesty now. Bitter shame
washed through her.

Teresa stood before her looking lovely and troubled.
It was impossible to imagine Nicholas touching this

other woman, but even so the blonde's presence was like a knife that slashed Eva from heart to gut.

Eva stood there, just looking at her, with no words to say.

Before Teresa could speak, Eva was rushing away.

The sky was vivid violet and gold. The Mediterranean had been painted with the same brush.

Nicholas found Eva hiding among the bleached piles of boulders on the remote windward side of the island. She had been huddled beneath the shade of a lone carob tree for hours, wanting nothing but to be alone. When he called her name, she didn't answer.

When he knelt and reached for her, she jerked away. "Don't touch me. Ever again. I couldn't bear it."

Then her fierce bitter tears began.

"So he's got to be mine, right?" Nicholas's jaw clenched and unclenched. "And you were the one woman who would stand by me."

"Just tell me one thing. What is Teresa's last name? And Nickie's?"

"Why ask, when you have it all figured out?" Nicholas said in a voice that was deadly calm. "It's Jones, of course."

Eva shrank against the white rock, trying to hide from him. "You're married. You have a child," she whispered. "No wonder you kept telling me we had no future."

"Eva! Damn it! Are you going to listen to me or not?" He took her hands, and held her against the rock. But when he saw himself tried and condemned in her eyes, he let her go.

"Teresa—what kind of woman is she that she can endure this kind of treatment? A saint?" Eva asked bitterly.

"Probably." Wearily he lighted a cigarette and shook out the match. He stared past her, scanning purple sky and sea for a long moment.

"You don't deserve a wife like her."

"No, I don't." He spoke in a flat unemotional tone.

"How could you mistreat a child...Nickie..."

He stamped out the cigarette in fury and disgust. He had inhaled only once. "Damn it. I couldn't. As always, when it comes to me, you see but you don't see. Teresa was the real Nicholas Jones's wife. Not mine, you little imaginative fool. When he died, there was very little insurance. I took care of her. I would have died but for him. When I built this house, I hired her brother to see after it. It seemed the least I could do."

"Then she's not your wife?"

"I told you she wasn't."

"How old is Nickie?"

"Eight."

"But he's so small. I thought he was five or six."

"You've been wrong—about a lot of things."

She stared bleakly into his eyes and saw nothing of him there for her. He was closed off, remote. Again.

"Don't stay up here too long," he said. "It's too dangerous. Too exposed."

The sun was sinking into a darkening sea as he turned to walk away.

She felt without life or breath as she watched him go. Weary from the tears and the emotion, she pressed her fingers to her eyes.

She wanted to call after him, but couldn't.

She knew she had lost him all over again.

Nine

After the cold way he'd been treating her, the last thing Eva expected was for Nicholas to smile and wave at her as he rowed the dinghy across the dark glimmering water toward *Rogue Wave*. She jumped up with barely concealed excitement and started to dash to the stern as eagerly as a puppy awaiting his master's return. Then she caught herself and salvaged a remnant of pride by walking with just a bit more reluctance.

But he had seen. Oh, yes he'd seen how her book had gone flying across the deck and nearly tumbled into the water.

Polishing chrome, pretending to read, she'd been waiting on deck practically the whole afternoon—waiting for him to return from the house. Hours ago he'd taken Victor and a briefcase full of papers up the cliff. To work, he'd said grimly, and to see if he could learn anything of von Schönburg.

At Nicholas's smile she'd felt the first flicker of hope in two days. Then she met his eyes and saw that they were as deep and as dark and as cold as ever.

For two long days she'd lived without his kisses, his smiles, his touches. Maybe that was why just the sight of him twisted her up in knots inside, that and the fact that he looked so heart-stoppingly handsome in a simple white T-shirt and tight jeans that molded his lean brown body to perfection.

He cut the engine and let the dinghy glide silently toward her. The slanting sun came from behind him and cast an iridescent gleam upon his black hair. The nearer he came, the more aware she was of a deep fluttering inside her breast, of her pulse racing out of control.

When she leaned down to help him secure the painter, he snapped the line out of her hand and looped it around the cleat by himself.

Her face froze. She turned away slightly, but not before he glanced up at her again and went momentarily still, his gaze roaming over her from head to toe, taking in the bright head with her feathery curls blowing in the faint breeze, her too brilliant eyes, her trim body in the tight lavender suit. Most of all he saw her tenderness and love for him flash fleetingly across her face, and suddenly he was vastly uncomfortable. He yanked his eyes away from her as brutally as he pulled and knotted the line he was tying.

"Where's Victor?" she dared to ask.

"He wouldn't come when I called him." Nicholas's reply was cool as he bent to stow the oars. "I have more important things on my mind than a cat."

"He won't just come. You have to go get him. You can't treat him like a dog."

"He'll climb down the path in the cave and yowl at us from the ledge when he's ready."

"That probably won't be till the middle of the night."

"He'd better come before then," Nicholas said abruptly. "Where's Zak?"

"Down below."

Nicholas and she were speaking to each other like strangers, trading necessary information with their carefully cool voices and polite sentences.

"He damned sure better have that transmission fixed."

Nicholas climbed up the ladder, managing to hold on to his thick briefcase at the same time. She expected him to walk past her.

But he didn't.

He stopped beside her, his great body coiled and tense. He was even smiling that terrible smile when his eyes stayed cold.

"Good news, *chère.*"

She went very still. Somehow she was sure it wouldn't be.

"The war between Otto and me is over."

"What?"

"The deadline for Otto's interest payments is past. He couldn't pay his creditors. More ships have been seized. His empire is collapsing like a house of cards. It looks like there will be immense international legal repercussions. He's cheated some pretty important people who are high up in governments. He's sold arms to the wrong people, too. Otto will be too busy talking to lawyers and trying to stay out of jail to take an interest in you. Since the story about Otto broke, your running away with me has made headlines in all the European papers.

"My men have informed the proper authorities of my real name, of the fact that I once worked for Otto, of the fact that it was I who was betrayed in Africa, of the fact that I own Z.A.K. World and am Otto's arch-rival. I think Otto is in such a tight spot he won't risk his own neck by allowing anything suspicious to happen to you. You can go home. Back to your shop, your world. Back to your safe, respectable life. Only it won't be quite so respectable after all the headlines. I'm afraid you may get a taste of what it's like to live with an unfairly deserved reputation."

In an agony she listened to him. Didn't he understand that her world had become one man? Didn't he understand that never again would she care about headlines?

"So, just like that it's over?" she whispered. "It's goodbye."

He would have walked past her, but she touched his arm. The onyx and gold ring on her right hand flashed. He jerked away from her.

"Do I mean nothing to you?" she pleaded.

He did not answer, but his eyes had fastened on her white face.

"How do I know I wasn't part of your revenge plan? How do I know you didn't just take me because you thought I was his? Maybe that was the only reason you made love to me—to get revenge!"

His face darkened, but when he spoke his voice was still calm, controlled. "You would think that," he said quietly.

As always her eyes were too easily filling with tears. "I don't think it. I just said it. I love you. I believe in you. This past week has been like a miracle. I never

want to go back. All my life I have wanted the one thing
you alone can give me—to be loved, truly loved.''

"No." He cut off her soft protestations of love. "It's
not in me to give anything more to you, and even if it
were, you'd never believe in me, *chère*. Maybe I have
Otto where I want him, but the damage he did me in
Africa will always be there between us. I can't ever be
the man I was before. No matter how all this comes out
there's no way I can ever completely clear my name. We
can't live on an island for the rest of our lives, cut off
from the world. There'll always be those who believe the
worst of me. If I married you, everything I was accused of would taint you, too. You have always wanted
approval.''

"I want your love."

"Maybe, but not enough to live without all the other
things you want as well. I'm not strong enough to give
you only part of what you need to have. I couldn't stand
for you to be my wife and doubt me. I can't be some
lawyer with some safe career. I'm not a Martin, I'm a
Girouard. And I have always lived differently than
you.''

Wife. Just the word made her want to weep. Before
her ghastly mistake about Teresa, had he actually been
thinking of marriage?

Eva had come so close, and that made everything so
much worse.

He saw the sparkle of tears still trembling on her
lashes. "Don't," he whispered. "You've always cried
too easily. Don't waste tears now when it was all over a
long time ago.''

Not for her. For years and years she'd grieved, she'd
put her life on hold.

"No...you're a part of me. If you leave me, that part will die."

"I *will* leave you, for your sake as well as mine."

It was no use. No use. He was too terribly disillusioned, and she had played a horrible part in his disillusionment. But she wouldn't beg. Not anymore. "When...when are we going?"

"Zak?" he shouted past her, relief in his voice that their conversation was over. "When will the transmission be fixed?"

"I think I've got it."

"It's about time." Nicholas turned back to her. "We leave in an hour."

Lonely black despair closed around her. "I have to go up and get Victor."

"Nickie went into the cave, and Victor followed him."

"That place gives me the creeps. The cliffs are so steep. Sometimes the footpaths are wet. The water—" she broke off, unwilling to even think about the water.

"I'll go then."

"No. You see to the boat. Sometimes it takes some doing to talk Victor into coming."

"Take a can of sardines," he suggested.

For a man who didn't understand cats, he was making progress.

"I want to say goodbye to Teresa and Nickie, too."

"Say it fast."

She saw all too clearly how anxious he was to be rid of her.

Then he was untying the dinghy for her, helping her cast off. She didn't know that he watched her row all the way to the beach, that he watched her until she disappeared high up in the rocks as she climbed the cliff.

But what he should have seen, he couldn't.

Eva was almost halfway up the cliff when she saw a boat hidden in the cove, but she couldn't see the owner of the boat. Tourists, perhaps. Oh, well, they had to be down there somewhere.

When she came over the top of the cliff, a sullen man with lush Mediterranean good looks dressed totally in black suede was there waiting for her with a loaded automatic pointed right at her face.

Paolo laughed at her when he saw the wild fear in her eyes. She shrank away from him. "I've been looking for you, *Signorina*. Everywhere."

Then he reached for her.

At his touch, she began to shake. When she tried to run, scrabbling desperately across the hard dry earth, she stumbled and fell. He grabbed her and slammed her back against a rock wall. Terror made her oblivious to the gun barrel against her cheek. She was like an animal, her nails clawing and tearing at his face, ripping into his black shirt.

"We've got the boy." He laughed softly. She could feel his hatred of her that contaminated every male pore in him. His laughter came again and again, rolling over her in waves that were viciously evil and hideously sensual.

They had Nickie!

Her hands fell away weakly from his dark face. Her nails curled into her own palms like talons, slashing deep, vivid half-moons into her soft skin. She allowed Paolo to lead her up to the house.

Paolo shoved Eva through the door beneath the white vaulted ceilings arching over the cool blue tiles. The inside of the house looked as though it had been hit by a hurricane. A couch was overturned. A lamp had been shattered. The Aubusson carpet was stained with blood. There had been a violent struggle, but it was over now. Otto was leaning back in a white chair, with the arrogance of a victorious warrior-king lounging on his throne. Behind him the view of the Mediterranean was magnificent.

Paolo pitched Eva down on those cold tiles at Otto's feet as though she were a thing to be sacrificed.

Their eyes wide with terror, Teresa and Nickie were huddled together near the door with Victor crouched nearby. Eva saw a dark bruise across Teresa's blond brow, and blood was on her cheek and her dress. The monsters had struck her. Then Eva saw Marcos—lying beneath the overturned couch, his great golden body as still as a corpse.

Otto stared down at Eva indifferently. "Let her go."

"What?" There was barely contained fury in Paolo's deep voice, but his brutal hand fell away.

"We took the wrong woman, you fool. We should have taken Mrs. Jones and the boy. Eva, go down and tell Raoul that we are here and that we have his woman and child," Otto commanded.

Like Eva, Otto had jumped to the wrong conclusion.

Paolo regarded Eva with blood lust and hatred burning in his eyes. He would never let her live. They would use her to lure Nicholas to his death, and then they would kill her and everyone else.

"Tell him to come alone and unarmed," Otto ordered, "or the boy and the woman will die."

Eva stumbled outside and was blinded by the brilliance after the darkness inside the house. She blinked as if to wish the nightmare away. When she opened her eyes, she saw Nicholas emerging from the cave. He had taken the elevator, but even the short climb necessary to come from the cave to the house made his limp more pronounced. He looked tired. He was unarmed.

"Go back!" she screamed.

"Stay right where you are!" Otto's voice was soft with menace.

Behind her Eva heard Paolo's evil laughter. He was dragging Nickie and Teresa out of the house.

"Well, well, *Liebchen,* it looks like you can stay and enjoy the party." Otto's feral gaze held her spellbound. His automatic was aimed at Raoul's heart.

Eva knew they were all going to die.

"You thought to ruin me, Girouard. You are not the only one with the desire for revenge. You made me. You destroyed me. But I'm not going down alone. I am taking you with me. But first, your woman and your child will die. Then you—and I promise, my friend, you will die very slowly."

"This is between you and me, von Schönburg. Leave them out of it," Nicholas said gravely.

Otto laughed.

"It was clever of you to find the island." Nicholas was deliberately stalling, deliberately trying to keep Otto talking.

"Eva radioed for help. She gave your position, your heading. Everything we needed. It was an easy matter then, after talking to Anya. She had seen a chart once on board *Rogue Wave* with this island marked on it. She wasn't quite sure of its location. But she was humiliated after you ran away with Eva. A woman scorned... Anya was quite anxious to help me find you. But we had to search a dozen islands before we spotted this one."

Nicholas looked at Eva, and she saw vivid anguish flare briefly in his eyes. Then it was extinguished by a flood of dark anger at this new betrayal.

"Nicholas, I didn't mean... It was days ago that I made that call! I promise you...."

He wouldn't look at her. His hard face remained frozen with dark rage, and she knew she had truly lost him. In this life. In the next, too.

Nickie's tiny hand fluttered into hers. His fingers clung. Victor curled his tail around her leg and began to yowl at her feet. She felt Nickie's pulse beneath her fingertips—the delicate throb of his young life.

Eva had made the radio call that had brought them to this. If she didn't do something, they would all die because of her. They would all be shot like Nicholas's men in Africa.

She had already lost everything. There was nothing more for her to lose. But the child... The black cave was less than thirty feet away.

Thirty feet. Logic told her it might as well have been a million, but something snapped in her tired desperate mind. She hardly knew what was happening when her body catapulted forward. She scooped up Nickie and, protecting the child with her body, she fled to the caves. Victor raced ahead of them like a black bolt.

Everyone else went crazy, too.

There were heated shouts.

And a spray of bullets.

Behind her. Everywhere.

The distance to the cave seemed endless. Her legs were leaden. Their speeding steps seemed to be long, gliding, weightless leaps in slow motion.

Bullets shattered the rocks ahead of her and at her feet. All around her. Something stung her arm, but she felt nothing. She saw blood spatter against white rock and didn't know it was her own. She just kept running. Slower, now.

She was a child again running beneath the cypresses with Noelle along the bayou. *Grand-mère* was there in her black dress, scolding them for playing in their white lace Sunday clothes. They were laughing now at their stern grandmother as she wiped their muddy feet so they could come inside Martin House. The picture changed and Eva wore a gown of gold. Raoul was bending over her in the candlelight in a New Orleans restaurant, his dark eyes filled with love as his hand slipped an onyx ring onto her finger.

The black entrance to the cave loomed one step away.

Another bullet splintered off stone. Bits of rock cut into her face. She heard Raoul's ravaged shout, his voice, above the others, calling her name.

Was he dying? She couldn't look back.

Her memories faded into a blur. They were as meaningless as her life.

Then she and the child were in the cool, all-enveloping darkness of the cave. Eva couldn't see anything, and it was Nickie who pulled her along the narrow path.

It was cold inside, so cold. If only she had Nicholas's key to the elevator.

But there was no way down except the path.

Her eyes adjusted to the darkness. She looked down and saw the sheer rock wall tumbling away into black nothingness. The rocks became slippery with her blood. She was feeling faint. The pain in her arm was searing now, and everything seemed to be slipping away. Too weak to go any farther, she collapsed against cold wet rock, nearly unconscious.

Then she heard Paolo's muttered curse and knew that Nickie and she were no longer alone in the cave.

Was Paolo there because he'd already killed Nicholas?

Paolo would kill the boy, too, if she didn't stop him.

She didn't know if Nicholas was dead or alive. If he was dead she wanted to die, too. But first she had to save Nickie. First she wanted to destroy this monster who had killed her love. Her emotions were so fierce and terrible they brought her back to consciousness. For the first time she could almost understand the darkness in Nicholas, the savage desire for revenge.

She rose to her feet and let Nickie lead her down. Paolo grunted and stumbled along behind them. He was getting closer. The path got narrower and narrower. The rocks were wet with condensation. Or was it her blood? She looked down and again faintness threatened to overcome her. If she fell, she would hit the jutting ledge beneath. The terrible water was a dark glimmer, a long way beneath her.

She caught the thick smell of her pursuer. Paolo was so close he could almost reach out and touch her.

Suddenly Victor squalled.

Behind her Paolo screamed a shrill scream that was filled with utter terror. He had stepped on Victor and missed his footing.

Paolo was falling, but as he did he lunged forward and hooked his arm around Eva's throat. If he was going to die, he was determined to take her with him. Then her screams were mingling with his as she slipped and fell with him.

His body struck the ledge beneath, miraculously shielding her from the blow. But the strength of mur-

derous life was in him even after that. His hard hand
held on to her neck crushingly.

They hit the water together, and his heavy body was
pulling her down, down.

The fingers around her throat kept squeezing, until
she saw red stars streaming before her eyes. Together
they slid through the water, their bodies falling and
twisting weightlessly together in a macabre dance of
death. It seemed to her that they fell forever down that
dark, wet tunnel that was without end.

The meaningless memories were coming again, only
this time they were all of Nicholas. She was in his arms
as he shielded her from the fury of the storm at sea. He
was making love to her in their hidden grotto on a bed
of wet sand. Then she saw his face as she'd last seen it—
hard with the bitter knowledge of her fresh betrayal.

The images were fading like the flickering shadows on
a movie screen when the light comes on. Only there was
no light. There was only endless darkness.

Nicholas was on the ground, his own blood filling his
eyes, attacking Otto like a demon.

Then Nicholas heard Eva's screams, and the terror in
them pierced all the way to his heart. Nickie came running out into his mother's arms. Eva was in the cave,
dying, and Nicholas could do nothing to save her.

The two men rolled over and over until they were
grappling on the edge of the cliff. Beneath them the
rock wall dropped away to the hard stone beach a
thousand feet below.

The death struggle seemed to go on and on. Then
Nicholas twisted violently and Otto was beneath him,
his silver head dangling over the face of the cliff. Nicholas was straddling him, pounding him to death. Nich-

olas's large hands closed ruthlessly around Otto's neck and he squeezed windpipe into bone so Otto couldn't breathe.

Nicholas knew a savage thrill as his fingers dug deeper into that dark thick throat, as he watched the feral eyes bulge and go blank.

Then Teresa was there with Nickie calling softly behind Nicholas, her hand tugging at his shoulders.

"Don't. Please, don't kill him."

"For Eva," Nicholas growled, his mind crazed, beyond reason so fierce was his desire for revenge.

"Let him live—for Eva," Teresa pleaded.

Nicholas's hands loosened ever so slightly around the thick neck. Nicholas saw his men in Africa, their red blood staining the sand. The stench of death was all around him. One of those men had been Teresa's husband. Nicholas remembered his own nauseating terror that he would be next when he'd lain in the dirt, unable to move, and Paolo had swaggered toward him with his bayonet drawn.

Otto had to die.

"Killing is his way, not yours." It was Marcos's voice this time.

Nicholas hesitated. He stared at the man beneath him, his heart raging with the savage need to do violence.

"He had Eva killed!" Nicholas muttered hoarsely.

"Maybe she's still alive," Teresa said. "It is no good to live for revenge."

"How can you say that? Your husband died because of this man."

"That's how I know."

Finally what she was saying penetrated his brain. For a long moment he remained frozen on top of Otto.

Then in a daze he pulled his hands from Otto's throat, leaving Otto gasping for air. Marcos leaned down with a coil of rope and bound Otto's wrists together. Then his feet.

As if in a trance, Nicholas watched him. For years he'd lived with one purpose—to destroy von Schönburg. And now he was face-to-face with the terrible realization that the woman he loved might be dead because of his fierce desire for revenge.

The woman he loved...

He saw her as she'd looked down at him when she'd rushed to greet him this afternoon—with her face glowing in the shadows and sunlight. The rays coming through the entrance of the cave had turned her hair to flame. She had never looked more beautiful. And what had he done? With cruel words he had crushed that look. Destroyed her love. He thought of her courage, how she'd taken Nickie and run. The bastards had shot her. He remembered her last terrorized scream.

Killing Otto didn't matter. His death could change nothing.

Only Eva. Only Eva. With her tenderness and kindness and passion she had shown him that there was still some part of him that believed in the beauty of life. She had made mistakes in their relationship, but so had he. If only she was alive, he would forgive her everything. She had tried to teach him what it meant to love completely, without qualification.

He had treated her so brutally.

If she was dead, it was his fault. Not Otto's.

Nicholas knew he would never forgive himself.

If she was alive he would have to spend a lifetime making it up to her.

"Call the police," Nicholas said roughly.

Then he was racing, despite his bad leg, toward the cave.

Eva was cold, so cold. Her right arm burned with excruciating pain. But she felt the warmth of the sun on her skin. She heard the roar of the helicopter. Most of all she was aware of the raspy beauty of Nicholas's low-timbred voice.

Nicholas and Zak were hovering over her.

Through her lashes she could see Nicholas, his hand-some face bloodstained and grim. She was afraid to open her eyes, afraid of the coldness and the darkness in his heart.

But she opened them anyway because she wanted to look at him just one more time before she released him forever.

She lifted her head. Oh, it hurt. Terribly. So much so that she couldn't quite suppress a moan.

Nicholas was staring at her when her lashes flut-tered.

She saw the blazing warmth of his love. She felt his anguish, too. And his forgiveness.

She moved her lips to comfort him, but no sound came out.

"Don't try to talk," he whispered.

He was smiling, and it was Raoul's smile. "I thought I had lost you and that I would never be able to tell you how much I loved you." He touched her hair that was all wet and tangled with grit from the beach. "Forgive me," he whispered. "Forgive me."

To her surprise she saw that there were tears in his eyes. For once there were none in hers.

"There is nothing to forgive, my darling."

The helicopter was landing on the beach. Nicholas knelt over her to protect her from the flying dust and pebbles. He was cradling her head in his hands and gently kissing her brow.

She closed her eyes, but she knew he was there.

At last he was hers. The future was theirs. No more ghosts to haunt them from the past. No more good-byes.

Nothing mattered except that she and Raoul would be together. Always. She felt his strong arms lifting her to carry her to the helicopter.

All she wanted was for him to hold her close, against his heart, forever.

And she knew that at last he would.

Epilogue

Raoul stared down into the crib that was fringed with blue lace. As always when he came into the nursery filled with musical toys and teddy bears, he felt a soft glorious wonder and a love that was unconditional and all-encompassing.

Nestled against soft blue sheets and blankets was his son, whose hair was fiery like his mother's. Whose eyes were as black and sparkling with devilment as his father's.

Andrew Wade Girouard. It seemed a long name for such a little boy.

Gently Raoul reached down to touch his son, and when he did, the baby's tiny hand curled trustingly around his big brown finger.

Spread out upon an antique rocker were a starched white christening gown and cap. Next to pristine lace was a lazy ball of black fur. Victor had come up to hide from the fuss.

When the nurse saw the cat she would probably shriek about black cat hairs, but Raoul wasn't about to disturb Victor. He had learned a long time ago that that cat had a way of coming in handy.

"Today's the big day," Raoul whispered to his son.

Downstairs there was the sound of children playing—shrieks of merry laughter. Noelle's two daughters raced through the house on a rampage.

"You're never going to knock over your mother's antiques and break her china, now are you?" Raoul said proudly.

Raoul didn't hear the door behind him open and close, nor the whisper of light feet across the blue carpet. But he caught the scent of honeysuckle.

He turned, and Eva was there, his wife, looking beautiful in green silk and pearls with her red hair flowing about her shoulders. Just knowing she was there made his happiness complete. She was the one person he loved above all else, even his son.

"You can pick him up," she prodded gently with laughter in her voice.

He still couldn't quite believe that.

"He's so small."

"He won't break."

"You keep telling me that."

Eva came to the crib and bundled the blue blanket around the child and handed him to his father, who cradled him a bit awkwardly but ever so gently in the crook of his arm. Together they all walked out onto the shady veranda.

The white columns of Sweet Seclusion gleamed through the hazy sunlight sifting through the dark green trees. Around the mansion was a freshly painted white picket fence upon which ivy and Carolina jasmine had already started to climb.

The family was gathered today for Andy's christening. The Martins had come even though they still couldn't quite accept a Girouard, especially Raoul, as one of their own, as their son-in-law. Zak and Zola had come. They were sitting in the summerhouse with Zola's little girl toddling at their feet.

Eva was an inveterate matchmaker. Raoul remembered how she had insisted that Zak come to London for the wedding. Naturally Zola had been there, too, to catch Eva's bouquet.

Raoul still couldn't believe that his lovely wife and his handsome son weren't all part of a dream. He had his home, and a family to share it with, everything he'd ever longed for since he'd been a child. He had assumed his real name, and they lived most of the time in London, but their vacations and summers were spent at Sweet Seclusion. Eva had her shop. She was as disorganized as ever. Running the shop was a constant challenge for her, but business was brisk.

There were still those who believed even the worst rumors about him. What hurt the most was the occasional accusing article that was written, the letter sent to him by the relative of one of his men who had died in Africa. Eva's family would probably never quite accept him. But none of these things mattered as much as he'd thought they would to either Eva or himself, because they had each other.

There had been great darkness in his life, and long years of emptiness when he'd lived only for revenge.

But Eva with her love had led him back into a world of light that filled every single one of his days with profound joy.

Above all things he trusted in her and she in him.

Who knew, perhaps in time even the illustrious Martins would come to accept him. Eva still wanted their approval, but more than that she treasured his love.

Carrying his son, Raoul led his wife from the deep shade of the veranda into the sunshine so that he could watch the light turn their hair to fire. They stood there basking in the brilliant warm light and in the glorious joy of their love for a long time. Beneath they heard children's laughter and all the rich warm sounds of familial happiness.

He felt Eva's fingertips that were like flame move against his skin. His hand tightened on hers, and he pulled her closer. She was a part of him. She was everything, the center of his world that was now as golden as the sunshine. Sometimes he was so happy he felt he would awaken and find that it was all a dream.

He heard her voice washing over him, caressing him with its husky sound. "I love you. I want to fill our house with children. Our children."

He remembered the long years of anguish and could not speak, but his eyes gentled with love as he held her.

With her at his side, he knew he could face anything.

*   *   *   *   *

Bestselling author NORA ROBERTS captures all the
romance, adventure, passion and excitement of Silhouette in
a special miniseries.

THE
CALHOUN WOMEN

Four charming, beautiful and fiercely independent
sisters set out on a search for a missing family
heirloom—an emerald necklace—and each finds
something even more precious... passionate romance.

Look for THE CALHOUN WOMEN miniseries
starting in June.

COURTING CATHERINE
in Silhouette Romance #801 (June/$2.50)

A MAN FOR AMANDA
in Silhouette Desire #649 (July/$2.75)

FOR THE LOVE OF LILAH
in Silhouette Special Edition #685 (August/$3.25)

SUZANNA'S SURRENDER
in Silhouette Intimate Moments #397 (September/$3.25)

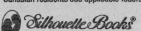 *Silhouette Books*®

Silhouette Special Edition®

proudly hails

WOMEN OF GLORY

from Lindsay McKenna

Soar with Dana Coulter, Molly Rutledge and Maggie Donovan—
Lindsay McKenna's WOMEN OF GLORY. On land, sea or air, these
three Annapolis grads challenge danger head-on, risking life and limb
for the glory of their country—and for the men they love!

May: NO QUARTER GIVEN (SE #667) Dana Coulter is on the brink
of achieving her lifelong dream of flying—and of meeting the man who
would love to take her to new heights!

June: THE GAUNTLET (SE #673) Molly Rutledge is determined
to excel on her own merit, but Captain Cameron Sinclair is equally
determined to take gentle Molly under his wing....

July: UNDER FIRE (SE #679) Indomitable Maggie never thought
her career—or her heart—would come under fire. But all that changes
when she teams up with Lieutenant Wes Bishop!

SILHOUETTE·INTIMATE·MOMENTS®

IT'S TIME TO MEET
THE MARSHALLS!

In 1986, bestselling author Kristin James wrote A VERY SPECIAL FAVOR for the Silhouette Intimate Moments line. Hero Adam Marshall quickly became a reader favorite, and ever since then, readers have been asking for the stories of his two brothers, Tag and James. At last your prayers have been answered!

In June, look for Tag's story, SALT OF THE EARTH (IM #385). Then skip a month and look for THE LETTER OF THE LAW (IM #393—August), starring James Marshall. And, as our very special favor to you, we'll be reprinting A VERY SPECIAL FAVOR this September. Look for it in special displays wherever you buy books.

MARSH-1

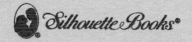

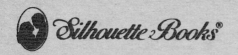
Silhouette Books®

SILHOUETTE BOOKS ARE NOW AVAILABLE IN STORES AT THESE CONVENIENT TIMES EACH MONTH*

Silhouette Desire and Silhouette Romance

> May titles: April 10
> June titles: May 8
> July titles: June 5
> August titles: July 10

Silhouette Intimate Moments and Silhouette Special Edition

> May titles: April 24
> June titles: May 22
> July titles: June 19
> August titles: July 24

We hope this new schedule is convenient for you. With only two trips each month to your local bookseller, you will always be sure not to miss any of your favorite authors!

Happy reading!

Please note: There may be slight variations in on-sale dates in your area due to differences in shipping and handling.

*Applicable to U.S. only.

SDATES-RR